"HE ISN'T DEAD, IS HE?"

Original illustration from the 1903 David C. Cook printing of Charles Sheldon's classic *Miracle at Markham*. Illustrator unknown.

# Miracle at Markham

# Miracle at Markham

CHARLES SHELDON

COOK COMMUNICATIONS MINISTRIES
Colorado Springs, Colorado • Paris, Ontario
KINGSWAY COMMUNICATIONS LTD
Eastbourne, England

Life Journey® is an imprint of
Cook Communications Ministries, Colorado Springs, CO 80918
Cook Communications, Paris, Ontario
Kingsway Communications, Eastbourne, England



Cover Design: Amy Kiechlin



First Printing, 2007
Printed in the United States of America

1 2 3 4 5 6 7 8 9 10

ISBN 978-1-58919-081-8
LCCN 2006933169

REV. CHARLES M. SHELDON.

Portrait of Charles Sheldon that appeared in the 1900 David C. Cook printing of *Robert Hardy's Seven Days*. Photographer/engraver unknown.

*About Charles M. Sheldon*

# Putting Faith into Action

❦

HARLES MONROE SHELDON—pastor, famous author, and tireless reformer—was a man who viewed Christian ministry and social activism as intertwined and inseparable. Contrary to many theologians of his day who regarded the practical ills of society as irrelevant to the task of winning souls, Sheldon believed Christianity would be considered irrelevant if it made no attempt to meet people's real needs and relieve suffering in tangible ways.

Near the end of his astonishing career, Sheldon was asked by seminary students to share his "tenets of ministry." He began as a pastor, he replied, with an "unquestioning faith in Jesus Christ as the one and only power in all the world, and the only one capable of saving the world." After more than thirty years of activist ministry, during which time he published thirty novels—including the classic *In His Steps*, one of the best-selling books of all time—it was clear that "saving the world" meant far more to Sheldon than an abstract theological concept.

"I define my Christ," he continued, "as the greatest statesman and economist of all time, and insist that legislation and education and political economy and industry look to Him as the one ... holding in His teaching the redemption of the world at every point."

In other words, Sheldon never saw a need or problem in the world that could not be remedied by the application of Christ's simplest teachings.

"Think on this," he wrote. "If men sought first the kingdom of God through Jesus Christ, they would have all the other material things necessary for human happiness."[1]

Sheldon's views reflected a larger movement of the time called "Christian Socialism." Although the word *socialism* would take on negative connotations in succeeding decades, at that time it meant addressing society's and individuals' needs and seeking practical ways to relieve hardship. Adherents of the movement emphasized leading a Christlike life and *doing* things to help people in Jesus' name.

Walter Rauschenbusch, a leader of the movement who credited *In His Steps* as his greatest influence, wrote that

Christ died to "substitute love for selfishness as the basis of human society."[2] That idea is the common thread that runs through Charles Sheldon's legacy of ministry and literature.

The great social upheaval of the latter decades of the 1800s—when Sheldon began his ministry—provided fertile ground for advocates of Christian Socialism. In the United States, the wounds of the Civil War were still fresh, and the country had to contend with the northward and westward migration of former slaves in search of a better life. Steel, petroleum, and electricity had propelled the Industrial Revolution, fueling massive change as factories drew workers from the countryside into rapidly expanding cities. Divisions between rich and poor stood in sharp contrast, and the labor movement was a powerful and unstable force confronting unfair and unsafe working conditions. Immigration altered the face of the nation, seemingly on a daily basis.

These issues all found their way into Sheldon's novels and influenced his philosophy of "untheological Christianity."[3] He believed that talking about God's love and grace without doing something to demonstrate them represented a shallow, hollow kind of faith. He consistently and unflinchingly brought these issues to life through his characters. Sheldon biographer Ellen Caughey wrote,

> Charles's novels, like other popular "social gospel" literature of the era, contained common themes. They were tributes to the middle-class working man, caught between the simpler days of rural living and the impending industrial modernization of the twentieth

> century. The differences between the rich and the poor, labor management and the struggling factory workers, and those who frequented barrooms and who were faithful churchgoers were emphasized. But his novels were filled with optimism, too. The future always looked bright whenever the protagonist decided to follow God's way and seek solutions found in the Bible.[4]

Sheldon's upbringing inspired him and prepared him to address themes involving the collision of rural and urban life as well as a moral versus immoral lifestyle. Born in 1857 to a Congregational minister and his wife, Sheldon moved with his family often during the first ten years of his life. The family finally settled down in 1867, when his father was named the Home Missionary Superintendent for the Dakota Territory, encompassing modern-day North and South Dakota. The family moved to a 160-acre homestead on the wide-open prairie outside Yankton. Indians were often seen camping in tepees at the edge of the family's property.

For young Charles, it was a life of adventure and hard work. All five Sheldon children shared equally in the task of running a frontier household isolated from civilization. Years later he wrote, "If there was anything that Dakota farm taught us all for life, it was the dignity and joy of work with our hands."[5]

Sheldon also learned to delight in using his mind and imagination. The need to provide one's own entertainment on the prairie created in him a lifelong love of books. At the end of each day, he could be found at the kitchen table with a kerosene lantern and his latest book, borrowed from a generous family friend in Yankton. He read Sir Walter Scott, Dickens, and Shakespeare. The family also read the Bible aloud each morning, starting over at Genesis every time they reached the end of Revelation.

Inspired by such a rich literary environment, Sheldon began writing stories of his own. By the time he left his prairie home to attend school in Andover, Massachusetts, several of his tales had been published in the Yankton newspaper, and he had even sold one to an East Coast magazine. On one trip to Boston as a student, Charles found a copy of *Les Miserables* in a bookshop he visited often. Without hesitation he bought the book, spending the money he needed for return train fare to Andover. After using his last few coins for a sandwich and cup of coffee, he walked twenty miles back to campus in a drizzling rain. His prize, however, remained dry, tucked away in his shirt.

After graduating from Andover Theological Seminary in 1886, Sheldon accepted the pastorate of the Congregational church in Waterbury, Vermont. There, he was determined to be the perfect example of what New Englanders expected in a minister. But it was there that he began to develop his conviction that Christian ministry must consist of action rather than mere spiritual theorizing. When he saw a need, he was compelled to do everything he could to meet it, even if his efforts had nothing to do with traditional evangelism.

For instance, it came to Sheldon's attention that many of the ladies in Waterbury complained about the amount of dust created by traffic on the town's dirt streets. It infiltrated their homes through open windows and coated the furniture. He went to work immediately and organized the construction of a pipeline from a nearby spring to a holding tank in town. Then he conscripted a townsman to drive a water wagon that sprinkled the roads to control the dust. A huge crowd turned out for the inaugural voyage down Main Street, and for the remainder of his time in Waterbury, Sheldon had devoted supporters among the members of the Ladies Aid Society.

Another time, Sheldon and a local physician conducted a study that linked a string of mysterious deaths in the town to contaminated drinking water where pig stalls were placed too close to wells. He also organized a church garden that became a profitable source of funds for the needy and for missions. He created a popular reading club for the town's young people, "something for them to do besides dancing and card-playing."[6] Sheldon went on to found the town's first library.

As much as Sheldon's time in Waterbury had done to shape his Christian Socialist theology, the town would play an equally large role in the young minister's personal life. It was there he met Mary "May" Merriam, whom he married in 1891. The couple would eventually have one child together, a son.

May's father facilitated Sheldon's move to the pastorate of a new Congregational church in Topeka, Kansas. Indeed, Sheldon was eager to return to the prairie of his childhood where the breezes, he wrote, "start somewhere in the Rocky Mountains and do not stop until they hit the Alleghenies, and begin to get discouraged only about the time they reach the New York Palisades."[7]

Sheldon wound up staying in Topeka for the next fifty-seven years. In 1889, at the inauguration of the Central Congregational Church building, he set the stage for his extraordinary ministry, declaring that the church would reveal "a Christ for the common people." Christ's religion, he said, "does not consist alone in cushioned seats, and comfortable surroundings, or culture, or fine singing or respectable orders of Sunday services, but [in] a Christ who bids us all recognize the Brotherhood of the race, who bids throw open this room to all."[8]

Along with his passion for ministry, Sheldon maintained his love for literature, particularly for writing stories of his own. In Topeka, he found a way to bring these two strands of his life together. Searching for a strategy to boost flagging attendance at Sunday evening services, he remembered the popularity of the book club he'd founded in Waterbury. He made a decision that was to shape his literary career for the rest of his life and even lead him to write *In His Steps.* Sheldon decided that, instead of preaching on Sunday evenings, he would write novels and read new chapters aloud each week. His first book—*Richard Bruce, or the Life That Now Is*—was an unqualified success, drawing ever-larger crowds, along with offers from publishers to print his stories.

If Sheldon's writing seems to be overtly instructive and moralistic to modern readers, there's a good reason: Virtually every novel and short story he wrote was first and foremost a sermon delivered from his pulpit. If readers in our more skeptical era find his tone "preachy," it is because he literally preached his material before adapting it to print form.

Whatever the criticisms about his writing, the strategy worked wonders. By all accounts, his parishioners found his spoken-word stories and parables thoroughly captivating. For Sheldon, this formula allowed him—and forced him—to produce at least one chapter each week, which added up to a novel or two each year. It was a method Sheldon employed to great effect for decades.

Meanwhile, Sheldon wasted no time making good on his promise to "throw open the doors" in his ministry. He announced a plan to identify eight sections of his city and then spend a week living among each of them, learning firsthand the needs of common people. Over the following two months, he immersed himself in the world of streetcar operators, college students, impoverished blacks, railroad workers, lawyers, physicians, businessmen, and newspaper workers.

The weeks spent among the African Americans in Tennesseetown—as the segregated section of Topeka was known—were to be the most important to Sheldon, giving shape to a new mission for his church. During subsequent years, he spearheaded numerous outreach projects among the thousand or so freed slaves living in Tennesseetown. There, he founded one of the first kindergartens in the country, a school that became a model for others across the nation. Furthermore, his church provided job training, established a library, led efforts to close down saloons and "speakeasies," created village beautification programs, planted new churches, and opened its own doors to black members (quite progressive and controversial at the time).

Sheldon wrote of these experiences in his novel *The Redemption of Freetown.* Fictional pastor Howard Douglass said,

> How shall we redeem Freetown? It is not an impossibility. It is not a vague dream of what may be. It is within the reach of actual facts.... The place can be saved. But it is God's way to save men by means of other men. He does not save by means of angels, or in any way apart from the use of men as the means.

Throughout his career, Sheldon was a vocal opponent of drinking, gambling, greed, corruption, and misuse of the Sabbath. Nearly all of his books—which were often autobiographical—confront these evils and place the burden of responsibility for social reform squarely on Christians. For instance, *Miracle at Markham* is partly set in Pyramid, Colorado, a rowdy mining town with a gambling problem. A young minister, Francis Randall, is determined to stamp the evil out.

> There were two sentences in [Francis Randall's] sermon near the close that struck William's mind like a blow: "Any Christian living in Pyramid today is a coward and is faithless if he does not do all in his power to confront this gambling curse. No one has any right to say it is none of his business."

To Sheldon, the whole point of Christianity was to lead a Christlike life, which he saw as the foundation of the kingdom of God on earth. He was impatient with anything less. To him, addressing poverty, injustice, vice, and wasteful living were not distractions from saving souls; confronting these and other issues represented a Christian's first calling.

This conviction led him to write the most influential four words of his entire career: What would Jesus do?

The novel *In His Steps: What Would Jesus Do?*—which would go on to sell more than thirty million copies worldwide—began like his other books, as episodes to be read on Sunday nights. In the story, Reverend Henry Maxwell faces a crisis when he fails to help a tramp who comes to his door asking for work in the church. Maxwell politely turns him away, "too busy" to do anything more. The following Sunday morning, the tramp shows up at Maxwell's church and makes another appeal, this time in public.

"It seems to me," the man says to the assembled congregation, "there's an awful lot of trouble in the world that somehow wouldn't exist if all the people who sing such songs went and lived them out."

Maxwell is stunned. He takes the man home with him, only to watch him die a few days later. Stricken with guilt at the man's rebuke, Maxwell makes this plea the following Sunday to his congregation:

> The appearance and words of this stranger in the church last Sunday made a very powerful impression on me. I am not able to conceal from you or myself the fact that what he said, followed as it has been by

> his death in my house, has compelled me to ask as I never asked before, "What does following Jesus mean?" ... What I am going to propose now ... ought not to appear unusual or at all impossible.... I want volunteers from the First Church who will pledge themselves, earnestly and honestly for an entire year, not to do anything without first asking the question, "What would Jesus do?" And after asking that question, each one will follow Jesus as exactly as he knows how, no matter what the result may be.

The story follows those who answer this call and details the difficulties they face and the sacrifices they must accept. It is an indictment of the compromises Christians make in the world of politics and commerce that often directly lead to suffering and injustice in the lives of common people.

The Sunday night readings of *In His Steps*, like his other stories, were a huge hit. Word of the book quickly reached the Advance Publishing Company in Chicago. The editors wrote to Sheldon offering seventy-five dollars for the rights to publish the story in serial form. Sheldon accepted the offer, despite advice from family members that he should seek out a company willing to publish the chapters altogether as a complete book. The immediate and overwhelming success of the series surprised everyone, perhaps the Advance Publishing Company most of all. In the rush to get the first issues to print, the company neglected to file the proper copyright paperwork.

It was soon discovered that Sheldon no longer held the legal rights to *In His Steps*. As a result, dozens of publishers hurried to the printers with their own versions, and Sheldon received little remuneration from the sales. The book could have made him a millionaire, but he never grew bitter about his lost fortune. Years later, he wrote, "The very fact that over fifty different publishers put the book out gave it a wide reading, and established its public as no other one publisher could possibly have done."[9] Before his death in 1946, Sheldon had seen the book translated into thirty-two foreign languages.

In 1912, after twenty-four years in the pulpit, Sheldon resigned as pastor of Central Congregational Church. Over the next several years, he crisscrossed the country and traveled the world as part of a vigorous campaign to promote the national prohibition of alcohol. He returned to his pastorate in Topeka briefly after the Eighteenth Amendment to the Constitution was ratified, but in 1919 he retired from the church for good. For several years thereafter, he was editor-in-chief of *Christian Herald* magazine. Never one to be idle, Sheldon remained active during his retirement years, writing, speaking, traveling, and participating in numerous ministry endeavors. He died in 1946, two days short of his eighty-ninth birthday.

Almost a half century later, Sheldon's words swept the United States again when *In His Steps* and its message of uncompromised Christian duty unexpectedly regained widespread popularity. Before long, "WWJD?" (short for "What Would Jesus Do?") showed up on countless T-shirts, bracelets, key chains, bumper stickers, bookmarks, and trinkets of every kind. One can only speculate about how Sheldon would have reacted to such a phenomenon. Would he have been pleased that his phrase piqued interest and prompted people to think about their actions? Or would he have lamented the commercialization of a genuine, heartfelt question for people of faith?

Whatever the case, Sheldon's words, spoken through his protagonist Henry Maxwell, seem more urgent today than ever:

> The call of this dying century and of the new one soon to be, is a call for a new discipleship, a new following of Jesus, more like the early, simple, apostolic Christianity, when the disciples left all and literally followed the Master. Nothing but a discipleship of this kind can face the destructive selfishness of the age with any hope of overcoming it.

Charles Sheldon preached and wrote about the world-changing power of the Christlike life. His greatest achievement is the proof he offered—in himself—that such a life is possible.

Notes

1. Ellen Caughey, *Charles Sheldon* (Uhrichsville, OH: Barbour Publishing, 2000), 189–90.

2. "The Theology and Writings of Walter Rauschenbusch," Georgetown College course syllabus, ed. Kyle Potter, http://spider.georgetowncollege.edu/htallant/courses/his338/students/kpotter/writings.htm.

3. Timothy Miller, *Following In His Steps*

(Knoxville: University of Tennessee Press, 1987), 187.

4. Caughey, *Sheldon*, 111.

5. Miller, *Following In His Steps*, 7.

6. Caughey, *Sheldon*, 55.

7. Ibid., 184.

8. Miller, *Following In His Steps*, 23.

9. Ibid., 99.

*1.*

# A Letter That Broke Two Hearts

ELL, JOHN," SAID THE minister's wife, coming into the study, "what does William write? I saw his letter. Please read it to me."

Reverend John Procter, pastor of the Congregational church in Markham, hesitated as he turned toward his wife with a letter in his hand.

"What's the matter?" she asked. "Is anything wrong?"

"It's a serious matter, Kate," John said, gravely. "Don't be alarmed. William is not in any danger. But you must be prepared for unexpected news."

He opened the letter but hesitated. Then he read aloud:

Dear Father and Mother,

I am aware that this letter may cause you some

> pain, and yet I have thought the entire matter out prayerfully, and I cannot avoid the result. To tell you at once what my news is, I will say I have decided to leave the seminary and give up my preparations for the ministry.

The minister paused a moment and looked at his wife. She had grown suddenly pale. "Go on, John," Kate said finally. She sat during the rest of the letter with her head bowed. Her husband read:

> You know that during the summer I have been filling the pulpit at Granby. I have written you about some of my experiences there, but I have not told you anything of my real experience.
>
> From the day I entered the seminary, the ministry has contained less and less that appealed to me. I have come to feel that the churches are separated and weakened by their foolish denominational pride. There is almost nothing in the ministry to attract a man who really wants to serve the world.
>
> The Congregational church has seventy-two members. They have had six pastors in twelve years, and none at present. They pay decent wages and provide a parsonage. I learned after I had been there two months that the church committee receives twenty-five or thirty applications a month from ministers who would like to candidate for the position.
>
> In Granby, there are eight churches to three thousand people. The Congregational, Baptist,

Presbyterian, Episcopal, Free-Will Baptist, Lutheran, Christian, and Methodist.

These all have separate church buildings and ministers. Besides these, the Christian Science people have meetings in a hall, and the United Brethren hold services every other week in the district schoolhouse near the railroad shops. All of these churches are in debt, and all but two are behind with salaries.

All this has made me feel that I can not honestly go on with my studies for the ministry. In fact, dear Father and Mother, I have lost my respect for the ministry as a profession and for the churches as organizations for doing Christian work.

You do not know what it costs me to write this. I know something of the pain it gives you. You have always thought of me as a minister. Dear Father, believe me, nothing but a feeling of profound conviction could make such a confession possible. But you have brought me up to tell the truth and be true to convictions, no matter what the cost. And I am compelled to confess that the condition of the churches, the fickleness and instability of the minister's position, and the unchristian division and sectarianism of the denominations have produced in me such a distaste and unfitness for the ministry that I must leave the seminary. I am prepared to give up the life that you and mother have so fondly planned for me these many years.

I do not know yet what I shall do for a living. I have often wished that I had learned a trade before leaving home to go to school. I am perfectly well physically and, if necessary, I can go out to work as a day laborer. In any case, Father, I do not wish you to send me any more money. If you do, I shall return it. I can take care of myself, somehow. You know that with all I have said, I have not lost my Christian faith. My experience has not shaken that. But I must exercise it somewhere else besides in the ministry. Give much love to Jane.

Your loving son,
William

There was a long silence in the little study. John could not conceal from his wife the deep disappointment caused by his son's confession. He thought of all the hopes and ambitions he had felt for this son's career. It seemed to him like disobedience, like treason, now that this son had turned his face against the ministry and the church.

Kate finally spoke. "What do you think, John? Has he good reasons for such a step?"

John was silent for a moment. The question his wife had asked him was one he could not honestly answer just then. The asking of it angered him.

"He is not old enough to decide such great questions so hastily," John said sharply.

Kate was silent for a moment.

"At least we must respect William's honest convictions," she said softly and with some pride. "He must be true to them."

"Even if he is false to us!" said the minister bitterly.

"You did not mean that, did you, John?" asked his wife, laying her hand on his arm.

"I would not have said it if I did not mean it," he replied. "William has deceived us. He should not have gone on all these years pretending."

"John, you cannot believe that!" cried his wife rising and coming up close to him.

"At least, his decision is—"

"Well, it doesn't mean a loss of love and respect for our boy," she interrupted. "It is a deep disappointment, but let's give him the benefit of trust in his convictions."

John suddenly looked up into his wife's face.

"I spoke hastily," he said with a sad smile. "Let's take time to think it over. Yet I wish this news had come later in the week. I am not in a very good frame of mind to write my sermon after this."

"Mother," called a voice from the kitchen, "please help me with this recipe, won't you?"

"Yes, Jane," said Kate. "I'll be there in a moment."

The minister's wife looked at her husband with tears in her eyes. He stooped and kissed her, and neither said a word.

When his wife had gone out of his study, John turned about to his writing desk and picked up his pen. He sat with it in his hand for a minute, but he could not think of anything to write.

Suddenly, he threw his pen down and rose and walked over to his window. From where he stood, he could see the main street of Markham and count five church steeples. He stood by the window for several minutes, and a look of scorn and disgust grew on his face.

"Is William right about it, after all?" He asked the question aloud, and walking away from the window, he took up his pen and began to write notes of his thoughts.

> Here in Markham, we have twelve churches to twenty-eight hundred people. We beat Granby by four churches. Seven of these denominations have their buildings on the same street within a few blocks of one another. This street is the best street in town. There is only one church building in the factory district. Nine of these twelve churches are, to my positive knowledge, in debt, six of them with mortgages on their property.
>
> With all these churches, we have a town with fifteen saloons, a notoriously corrupt town council, the mayor of which is the owner of most of the saloons, and an increasing population of factory workers whose children run the streets and recruit the criminal classes. Our Sunday laws in Markham are contemptuously disregarded, relatively few observe the Lord's day, and drunkenness and vice are common.

The reverend lifted his pen from the paper where he had written and paused a moment. Then he added: "Markham is well churched, but where is Christ?"

He threw his pen down and rose and walked over to the window again, leaving the sheet of paper over the leaves of his partly written sermon.

"William is right about it, after all," he said out loud, though he was alone in the study. "How much is there in the ministry to attract a young man with Christian ambitions—a young man who really is eager to serve his fellow man? How much influence do these twelve churches have in Markham? I don't blame you, William, I ..."

John walked away from the window again and sat down at his desk. The look on his face had changed again. Since his son's letter and the feeling provoked by it, he had grown visibly troubled. The lines in his strong face had deepened, the care in his eyes had grown more defined. After all these years, how had Christ's prayer been answered? Were His disciples one? Could they ever be made one? His thought finally narrowed to Markham. Was it possible for the churches in his town to be unified? Could Christ ever be made the real Master of these divided bodies?

John drew another sheet of paper toward him, and after a little hesitation, he wrote the following: "Possibilities of uniting the twelve different denominations in Markham." Beneath that heading, he listed the pastors of Markham, with a brief description of each. He ended by writing about himself:

> Congregational church, Rev. John Procter, pastor. Graduate of academy, college, and seminary. Unduly proud of that fact. A man of strong passions, who thinks all the other churches ought to be Congregational in order to be truly united. Fonder of reading than of making parish calls. Preaches generally from manuscript and does not feel at his ease before a

crowd of working people, though willing to face them and do the best he can. Is at present the oldest resident pastor in Markham, having lived there fifteen years.

John smiled grimly while writing his own biography. Then he read what he had written about the other ministers, and after finishing, he slowly but carefully tore the sheets of paper in pieces and threw them into the wastepaper basket.

"I have no right to judge them," he said aloud. "I have no doubt they are all better, more Christian men than I am. And yet I believe I have fairly given their principal characteristics as ministers. Is there any power on earth that can unite such a body of men? What can ever bring together two such churches as the Baptist and Episcopal? Dean Randall and Harris are as opposite as any two men I ever saw. They are as likely to mix as oil and water. When I think of church union, the real kind, in Markham, I am obliged to think of a miracle. Would even a miracle unite such men and such churches? And yet we all claim to be alike—fellow Christians. Why are we not all doing Christian work together as Christ prayed we might?"

He rose and walked up and down, restless, unable to throw off the questions he had asked. He reread his son's letter, and the anger he had felt at his first reading was now gone. A deep sadness filled his heart.

"If the churches ever really unite, it will be by a miracle," he said repeatedly. When Kate gently knocked on his study door to announce dinner, John was still sitting at his desk, but his head was bowed over the pages of his unfinished sermon.

2.

# A Conversation in the Kitchen

HILE JOHN WAS STEWING and ruminating in his study that morning, his wife and daughter were having an interesting conversation in the kitchen.

Jane Procter was one of the teachers in the public schools of Markham. It was the last week of vacation, and she was spending the time at home, helping her mother with housework.

When her mother came into the kitchen, Jane saw at once that something unusual had happened. She was as curious as most girls, and after the dinner was put in the oven to bake, she said, “What’s the matter, Mother?”

Kate told her the contents of William’s letter, adding, “Of course, your father and I cannot help feeling very much grieved by it. We have never thought of Will as anything else but a minister. Your father will take it harder than anyone.”

"Mother," said Jane after a moment of silence, "I don't blame Will at all. Isn't what he says about the churches in Granby true of thousands of towns and cities all over the country? Why should Will be one more man to struggle to get a little church and then struggle once he's got it?"

"It's what his father and his before him have done," sighed Kate. "It is the noblest profession there is."

"Except teaching, Mother," Jane chided. "The average church touches children once a week, but the school touches them five days a week."

Her mother did not reply.

"Don't you think that the ministry offers very little nowadays to a young man of any strong ambitions?" Jane added.

"It is a life full of service," replied Kate, proudly.

"Yes, but it is so full of wasted strength."

"I don't know about that," Kate said. "There is a good deal of wasted strength everywhere. But surely, Jane, you can't help feeling some sorrow at William's decision."

"Frankly, I don't feel a bit," she said. "I honor Father and his work, of course, but it seems to me the life of a minister is not very desirable. Just look at the ministers in Markham. They—"

"Jane," said her mother, with a little of John's decided tone, "you must not judge."

"I'm not judging," said Jane calmly, picking up the rolling pin and using it unconsciously to gesture with. "I was simply going to compare. But I won't even do that. One thing is for sure, Mother: I shall never marry a minister."

"Has any one of them ever asked you to?" Kate questioned.

Jane blushed and began, in some confusion, to scrape the

dough from the kneading board until she scraped down into the wood. Finally, she turned her head toward her mother and said, “You know that Francis Randall has asked me twice.”

“No, I have never talked with you about this before,” Kate said. “I might have suspected. But how was I to know? Your father and I have always believed in giving you all the freedom that we think a Christian girl ought to have.”

“Francis asked me last winter—just before going back to his church, after Christmas,” Jane responded. “I said no. He wrote to me again last spring. I answered him the same.”

Jane’s voice had grown steadier now, but her face was still flushed, and she rose and nervously began putting away the baking things.

“Do you love him?” Kate asked the question simply, just as Jane was going into the pantry.

“I’m afraid I do,” answered Jane, after a pause, and her mother did not see the tear that dropped into a teacup before Jane placed it on the shelf.

“Why should you be *afraid* that you do?” Kate asked with a slight smile.

“Because I have made up my mind never to marry a minister.”

“But Dean Randall’s son is a fine young man,” Kate said.

“Yes, I know,” Jane replied.

“He is very handsome.”

“Indeed, he is,” murmured Jane, bending her head lower.

“And you say you love him?” Kate repeated.

“I have never told him so,” replied Jane, softly, “and I never shall.”

"Jane," said her mother, "if you do not marry the man you love, whom will you marry?"

"I'm going to remain single," said Jane, and her voice trembled a little as she said it. "I'm just going to be a plodding, patient schoolteacher as long as I live."

"You are twenty-three years old," her mother replied, "and you must decide this question for yourself. But you would not respect Francis Randall if he were to give up his profession of the ministry to please you."

"I would despise him," said Jane promptly.

"And yet you say you love him, and nothing but the fact that he is a minister keeps you from marrying him?"

"I don't know that I love him so very much after all," said Jane, a little stubbornly. But her look contradicted her voice.

Kate opened her lips to say something, but at that moment the bell rang, and she went to the front door. When she came back, Jane had gone upstairs and the conversation was not renewed.

At lunch that day all three were absorbed in the events of the morning, but not much was said. When the meal was over, John went out to do some parish work.

Jane, after helping in the work of the kitchen, went to her room again. She sat down by a small table, and after a moment of hesitation, she opened a drawer and took out of it a letter and a photograph. She read:

Miss Jane Procter,

It is almost six months since I asked you to share your life with me, and this letter is simply to tell you that I have not been able to accept your answer as final. You know well enough that I love you wholly, as a man should who asks a woman to be his wife. I am in doubt as to your real feeling toward me, Jane, but if you do love me, nothing ought to keep us apart. You said you would never marry a minister. I am sure you would never become my wife if I left the ministry, and you know me at least well enough to know that I can never abandon the choice of my life work.

But I need you. That sounds selfish. If you love me at all, you will understand how far from selfish it is. Won't you, can't you, marry me, Jane? My little church here is in the midst of a rough mining camp, and my salary is small. But I have a growing income from my little stories. I can make two people very comfortable even out here.

There was something in the way you said no last Christmas that made me feel I might some time hear you say yes. That is my only excuse for writing to you. If you will consent to marry me, no man will be happier or prouder, or more thankful to God.

Yours sincerely,
Francis Randall

She looked directly at the photograph and said aloud, "No, I will never marry you, sir. I am not fit to be a minister's wife. A little Episcopal church in a new mining camp out west! Jane Procter, it would be foolishness. You always said you would not marry a minister. I can't. I won't. But I do love him—even if I said I would never tell him so!"

She suddenly snatched the photograph from its prominent place on the table and thrust it into the drawer and shut it. And then she spread the letter out on the table and laid her cheek upon it and cried softly.

---

In John's study, there was a real struggle going on in the heart of the minister. The letter from his son had stirred emotions that lay deep and strong in the older man. The problem of the town that he had grown to love through his long residence in it had never before stood out so sharply as today.

He had given up the text and subject of his sermon and was planning something entirely different for the coming Lord's Day.

He stood by the windows and watched the moon rise. It came up behind a church steeple that stood out sharply against the yellow disk. It was the steeple of his own church. When the moon passed out of sight, John turned away and thoughtfully walked up and down for a long time.

*Can these ministers and churches be brought together?* he thought. *Can it be done without a real miracle? How shall it ever be brought about? Can Christ's prayer be answered here in this place, and His servants, His disciples, be one, even as He was with the Father?*

3.

# Dean Randall Receives a Letter

❦

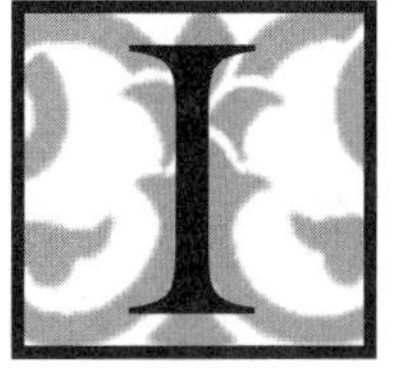

T WAS THE MORNING AFTER John Procter received the letter from his son, and Dean Randall was reading in his study in the mansion that was built close by the cathedral.

Dean Randall was a middle-aged man, well built, with a churchman's face and dress. No one would ever mistake him for anything other than a clergyman. There was, however, nothing pious or pompous in his appearance. It was said in Markham that he stood a good chance sometime of being made a bishop.

He had been reading for an hour and had laid the book down to do some writing when an assistant brought him a letter.

It was said long afterward that, among the many

astonishing things that occurred in Markham that winter, the coincidental arrival of two short letters, written by two young men, each to his minister father, had much to do with the unfolding of the momentous events.

The dean opened the letter quietly, but he had not read far when his face showed signs of deep feeling. The letter was from his son, Francis.

Dear Father,

I have already written you an account of this mining camp and my church work and of the people who make up my parish. But I have not told you much about my relations to the other churches here.

There are around twelve hundred people in Pyramid at present, and the place is rapidly filling up. There are six church organizations: Congregational, Presbyterian, Baptist, Methodist, Catholic, and my own. The Baptist and Methodist people have no church buildings but meet every Sunday in a storeroom, one denomination in the morning, the other in the afternoon, in the same place.

But the reason I write this particular letter is to tell you a little of my experience with one of the other clergymen. I met with an accident a month ago. I wrote you nothing of it because I did not wish to alarm Mother.

The mountains all about here are full of prospecting shafts. In crossing over the range one night to see a sick miner, I fell into one of these shafts. Fortunately, it was not deep, but I sprained my ankle and was severely bruised. I might have lain there uncomfortably all night, if I had not been found by the Congregational minister who had been out on a similar errand. To make a long story short, he succeeded in getting me into his own house, where I am now staying.

This little accident is but an incident in the whole course of events, and yet it has had something to do with my changed views about church matters. You know I never felt the importance that so many of our clergymen have felt—of emphasizing the ritualistic part of our church life. Since having a church of my own in this wild mining camp—with a parish that calls for a very plain service—I have come to regard less and less the ceremonies and traditions of our church and to feel more and more the longing to simply give this parish the thing it most ought to have—the gospel of daily bread for daily needs.

You will be startled now, Father, by what I tell you. Last Sunday, I invited the Congregational minister to preach to my people in my church. His building has been undergoing some repairs and could not be used. My lame ankle, which has been slow to heal, made it impossible for me to leave my friend's house, so that I could not be present at the service. I have heard, however, that the people enjoyed a good sermon. He read the prayers, and the service was the same as usual, except that he did not wear a robe in the pulpit. He offered to do so, but as he is a rather small man, and I am over six feet, and there is only one robe in the church wardrobe, it seemed foolish to insist on such an unimportant thing.

I understand there has been a little talk about this. Some of my people think it was very irregular. They have only words of praise for the sermon, however. It was practical and helpful to everybody.

I have been thinking, as I lay here in this little room, and growing to like the Congregational minister and his wife more and more, if there is not some way in which our two churches can unite more closely to do the work. Exchanging pulpits is a small matter. It might or might not mean a real union of church life. I have talked it over with Mr. Clark. He is ready to work with us in any service to the whole camp. I am sure we can accomplish much more together than separately and possibly prevail on the other churches to enter upon the same fellowship.

I do not know how much you can sympathize with me in this matter. I have no doubt you are disturbed by a part of this letter. If so, it is simply because I have frankly told you my inmost thought. The Episcopal church means less to me every day than the Christian work that the church ought to do. I find in my correspondence with the younger men in our denomination, that many of them feel as I do. We are entering a new period of church history, and I believe that the next twenty-five years will witness great changes in the customs and traditions of our own church.

There is one other matter I have had in mind to write you about for some time. I love Jane Procter, the daughter of your neighbor, John Procter, and have asked her to be my wife. She has refused to marry me because I am a clergyman. Her refusal has not changed my feeling for her in any way. You urged me, in your last letter, to have a home of my own even for the good of the parish and myself. Your letter led me to believe that you know nothing of this part of my life. I shall never marry anyone but Jane Procter.

If I have hurt you in any way by anything in this letter, it is more painful to me than to you. A young man is apt to think that he knows more and better than his elders. But I am positively sure that for myself the value of much that our church has counted dear in the past is rapidly passing away. I see more clearly every day the needs of the souls of men. Regardless to a great extent of past forms and customs, I am determined to go on in my ministry with the one fixed purpose of building up the kingdom of God rather than the Episcopal church. If this shall mean a vital and even organic union with all the other denominations, I shall welcome it as I would welcome a personal visit from Jesus Christ.

Your affectionate son,
Francis

Dean Randall held his son's letter in his hand for a long time after he had finished reading it. At first, Dean Randall was affected very much as John Procter had been—he was disturbed and even angry. Never once during his own ministry of over thirty years had he dreamed of inviting into his pulpit a clergyman of another denomination. It seemed to him like a breakdown of church order to think of such a thing. He had always been on good terms with the other ministers, but his relations with them and their churches were for the most part purely social, never religious.

That confession, however, did not affect him so disagreeably as his son's attacks on all the traditionally accepted customs of the Episcopal church. Could he, Dean Randall, ever think of uniting with any other church in Markham?

The favorite picture in his study was of Christ at Gethsemane. It hung just above his writing desk. An impulse he could not explain led the dean toward this picture now. Sometime near to that moment in Christ's life, He had prayed the great prayer that His disciples might be one. The dean could not believe that Jesus was thinking of the advancement of any particular church but of the kingdom of God on earth.

He looked away from the picture, and his eyes rested on a bundle of letters in one of the pigeonholes of his desk. Among those letters was one from a very powerful and influential member of the order of bishops in his diocese, in which he gave Dean Randall the assurance that he would be chosen as bishop in the near future. Clergymen, as well as politicians or other men, have their ambitions.

This was the ambition of Dean Randall's life—to become a bishop. His son's letter disturbed this dream. If the Episcopal church and its traditions were to become secondary in Dean Randall's parish, to the building of God's kingdom by union with other Christian bodies, what would become of that chance for the bishop's office? There was no hope of receiving that honor unless he remained faithful to the established traditions of the Episcopal church.

The dean was not willing to face the question in that uncompromising manner. He felt the need of putting off the whole matter. He rose, opened his study door, and called for his wife. She came in from the dining room, and the dean gave her the letter without a word.

The study door was ajar, and the servant at work in the dining room heard Mrs. Randall exclaim, "What! The poor boy! He fell down one of those horrible mining shafts? He must be badly hurt or even killed."

The servant listened carefully but heard only a low reply made by the dean, which she could not make out. Then the study door was shut, and only the murmur of the two voices from within reached her ear.

She went out into the kitchen just as the market man came into the back porch, and while he was taking some vegetables out of his basket, she said, "Have you heard the news? Mr. Francis fell down one of the mines out in Colorado and was probably killed. I just heard Mrs. Randall say so, in the study. She's in there now with the dean. They had a letter from Pyramid this morning."

"You don't say," said the market man, sympathetically. "Well? That'll be a blow to them. Young Mr. Randall was a likable lad. There's no telling what risks folks run in those Western mining towns."

"That's true," said the servant as she picked up the vegetables and went into the house.

The market man went his way with a bit of interesting news to pass along with his fruit and vegetables. He soon stopped at Reverend Procter's house, for the two ministers lived in the same block. Kate did not keep a servant, but a churchwoman was at the parsonage that morning helping with housework.

"You don't say," she exclaimed, as she stopped her work and faced the market man. "Poor fellow! Terribly mangled, you say he was? I'm sorry for his father and mother."

"What's that, Mrs. Brown?" asked Kate coming out into the shed. Jane was just inside the open kitchen door washing the breakfast dishes.

"Why, ma'am," said Mrs. Brown, eager to spread her news, "Mr. Francis Randall, the dean's son, out at Pyramid, was killed by falling down one of those mines out there. Killed instantly. His folks got the news—"

There was a sudden crash of broken crockery as Jane dropped the dish she was wiping. The next minute, she appeared in the shed, her white face trembling as she seized Mrs. Brown by the arm.

"Who said so?" she asked in almost a fierce voice.

"Ask him," said Mrs. Brown pointing in a frightened way to the market man who was just going out of the yard.

Jane rushed out of the shed and did not heed her mother's cry, "Jane! Jane! Come back. Perhaps it is not true."

"Who told you?" she asked the man.

He paused by his wagon in wonder at her sudden appearance and strange manner. "Told me what?"

"Who told you that Francis Randall was killed?" Jane demanded.

"I heard it straight from the girl at the Randall house. She heard Mrs. Randall say—"

But Jane was gone down the sidewalk, running with gasps and sobs toward the Randalls', crying as she ran, "Oh, it can't be true! It can't be true!"

The dean and Mrs. Randall were still in the study talking over their son's letter when they heard the front doorbell ring. A moment after, voices sounded in the hall. Then there was a sudden knock on the study door, and when the dean opened it, to his amazement Jane Procter confronted him and his wife, crying out hysterically, "He isn't dead, is he?"

"Who isn't dead?" asked the dean stupidly, but Mrs. Randall caught Jane's arm and drew her to herself.

"No, no, he isn't dead," she reassured. "Who said so?"

Jane fell into her arms sobbing out something they could not understand. The dean picked up his glasses, which had fallen on the floor in the excitement, and with a slight smile on his scholarly face, he patted Jane on the head.

Jane stopped crying, but after a minute of silence she looked up and whispered to Mrs. Randall, "You're sure he isn't fatally hurt?"

"There's his letter." Mrs. Randall held it out. "I think his father and mother are more dangerously hurt than he is," she added with a sideways look at the dean.

"Oh," said Jane, looking up and glancing at the dean. He had turned around and was pretending to be busy with something at his desk. Mrs. Randall put an arm around Jane and walked with her out of the study into the music room.

The two women had a little talk together. It is not quite clear whether Jane felt better or worse for her outburst of feeling. Mrs. Randall had tears in her eyes when Jane finally went away.

As for Jane, she walked slowly home. On the way, she said once, “If he had been killed … but no, I can’t, I won’t …”

So when the school term opened the next week, Jane went back to her old work, but as she listened to the droning of the children’s voices in the schoolroom, she often had a vision of the pale face of a tall young man sitting with a bandaged foot in a Congregational minister’s house out in Colorado.

4.

# William Leaves Andover

BOUT A MONTH AFTER THE letter from Francis Randall had caused such a disturbance in the family circle of two homes, John Procter came in late from parish calls with another letter that he read aloud to his wife and Jane at the supper table. It was from William.

> Dear Father, Mother, and Jane,
>
> I have at last made up my mind to leave Andover and try my fortune, for a time at least, in one of the mining camps of Colorado. I have tried a number of things here and can't make a go of any of them. A son of one of the professors here is part owner of the ore reduction mills at Pyramid. He wants a man who understands chemistry to act as assistant superintendent in the mill. I have asked for the position if it is still open,

and if it is I shall be on the way inside of a week.

Please don't feel that my life is a failure or anything of that sort. The work I am going into now is totally different from all you have dreamed of for me, but I believe it is all I can do just now. I would rather you not say anything to Dean Randall's family about my going to Pyramid. Of course, I know their son is there. The way I feel now, all tangled up in my mind, I would rather not meet him. I should be sure to say something to hurt his churchman's feelings. Anyway, in that little camp, I may run across him soon anyway.

The hard physical work will, I hope, make a man of me again. In any case, I do not want you to feel deeply disappointed in the way I have turned out.

Love,
William

John said very little. Kate cried over the letter, but Jane felt a variety of emotions. There was another part of her life in that mining camp now, though she was honestly puzzled to know why her brother did not want to meet Francis Randall.

"I'll answer the letter and take it down to the post office before the mail goes out," said John. "It will reach Will before he starts west."

"It seems strange that he does not say anything about stopping to see us on his way," Kate said sadly.

"That's exactly what I was going to urge him to do," said John.

He wrote a serious, loving letter to his son. He did not say one word of reproof or condemnation. But he urged him, for his mother's and Jane's sake, to stop at Markham on his way west.

---

The letter reached Andover the day before William was to start. He had been given the job in the mill, and there was no hesitation in his mind about going. But the letter from his father touched him. He thought it over that night, and the next day he bought his ticket with a stopover at Markham.

John was at the station to meet him when the train came in. People on the platform saw a rather slight, pale young man come down to meet the older one. The young man greeted his father with a simple, "Nice to see you. How are you doing?"

"I'm glad to see you, too, William," said the older man.

Inside the parsonage, William showed more emotion when his mother and Jane met him and kissed him. The tears were in his eyes as he took off his coat and hung up his hat in the familiar hall.

On the first night of his visit, William was in his old room upstairs unpacking some things from his trunk. Jane came in just as he was pulling out a package of letters and photographs.

"Want to see some of my seminary classmates?" he asked, as he handed her the packet.

Jane sat down on the floor by the trunk and began to take out the pictures. William continued his packing.

"Do they let girls study for the ministry at Andover?" Jane asked.

"What's that?"

"Is that one of your classmates at Andover?" Jane asked, as she turned the face of an attractive-looking young woman toward William.

"Give me that!" cried William with a rudeness so unusual for his gentle spirit that Jane was hurt by it.

She handed him the photograph and rose to leave the room, but William called her back.

"Don't go, Jane. I'm upset, that's all. I thought I had lost the picture. I want to tell you something."

Jane's curiosity was stronger than her momentary feeling of hurt, and she came back at once and sat down by the trunk again.

"That is the face of the girl I love," said William, gravely.

"I don't see anything dreadful about it, Will. She looks like a very nice girl."

Will was silent. He turned to the trunk again.

"Tell me, Will," said Jane, putting an arm around his neck as she sat by him.

"There isn't much to tell," said William in a muffled voice, as he threw a book into the trunk. "We were engaged, and when I changed views about going on with the ministry, she, well, we talked it over and agreed it would be wiser to break the engagement. She said she could not marry me if I was not going to be a minister."

"How funny that is!" exclaimed Jane, suddenly.

"I don't see anything funny about it," said William gloomily, as he turned away from his sister.

"Oh, but it is," replied Jane. "Because, you see, this girl won't marry you unless you are a minister, and I have made up my mind never to marry anyone who is a minister. If we could only straighten things out. They seem so mixed somehow."

"Have you been disappointed in love too?" he asked.

"No," said Jane. "I'm not disappointed. That isn't the word." But she would not tell William anything more, and after finding out that the Andover girl was a daughter of one of the professors and also a teacher in the public schools, like herself, she went out and left William to himself.

"Girls are so strange," he said, as he finished his packing. The missing photograph did not go back into the trunk, but into an inside pocket.

During the days that followed, John Procter and his son had some earnest talks together. There had been a secret hope in the father's mind that his son might reconsider his determination to leave the ministry forever.

"I don't deny, Will," his father said at one point, as they sat in the study during one of their many discussions, "I don't deny that the church of Christ in the world is far from being what He prayed it might be. But do you really think it will advance the kingdom of God by abandoning the church and trying to do Christian work *outside* instead of from *within*?"

"I cannot decide for anyone else, Father," said William, and his intense blue eyes spoke of a resolution that could not be changed. "It is pointless for me to think of doing my Christian work in a pulpit. I would fail, as any man ought to fail who tries to work where his heart is not in it."

John sighed and gave up all effort after that conversation to change his son's views. The only approach he made to the subject again was just before William stepped on the train that carried him west.

"You can preach from the pulpit of your mill out there," John suggested.

William knew what he meant. He replied as he shook hands. "That's true, Father. I haven't lost my faith in Christ as Master, even if I have lost faith in the church as my workshop."

---

William had been in Pyramid two weeks and was beginning to get acquainted with his new duties in the mill when Francis Randall paid him a visit.

William was dressed in his workman's clothes and, like every other man in the mill, was covered with dust and grime. The operation was all quite strange to one who had never seen such things: the rattle of the machinery; the glow of the mixing carriage as it regularly emerged from its white-hot furnace and rolled on its circular track radiating its intense heat as it traveled ceaselessly around; the splashing of the chemical stream running over the zinc reservoirs.

William had stepped to the door of one of the large vat rooms and was standing there enjoying a breath of fresh air. He had inhaled more than the usual chlorine gas that afternoon, which gave his face a pallor almost like one in a dead faint.

As he stood in the door, Francis came up, and before he had time to draw back into the vat room, the clergyman had put out a hand, saying, "Glad to see you, Procter. I heard from one of the Andover professors, a friend of Father's, that you were here." Then he added as he saw William's face closer in the evening light, "You're not sick, I hope."

"Nothing serious," William replied. "I've taken in a little more chlorine than is good for me. Excuse me for not shaking hands. These rubber gloves don't come off easily."

The two young men stood talking a few minutes by the door, and then Francis prepared to leave.

"I'll be very glad if you'll come and see me," said Francis. "I'm staying with Mr. Clark, the Congregational minister. I have a room there. If you want any books at any time, my library is at your disposal."

"Thank you," said William. He did not say that he would come, and Francis did not appear to notice it. Nevertheless, William decided right then to go and hear Francis preach the following Sunday.

---

Meanwhile, Dean Randall was unable to throw off the impression made by his son's letter. In spite of his attempt to forget it, the struggle in his mind grew. It finally narrowed down to the plain question of his personal ambition to be bishop and the opportunity to use his church for the growth of Christianity. His own ambition and the cause of Christ were finally in open and unmistakable conflict.

It must be said this result had not been reached suddenly. Dean Randall's experience for several years had been silently and slowly shaping matters. His son's letter was only one additional influence. But while the people in his parish never dreamed of any struggle in the life of the scholarly, reserved Episcopal clergyman, there was daily growing in him a conflict between personal ambition and the worldwide power of the cross.

Three weeks after receiving his son's letter, the dean's conflict had reached a crisis. How momentous, not even he knew. But he was soon to have the clearest and severest test made of his church life.

The dean was in his study Friday night. It was late, but he kept on studying and writing. Outside, the wind was blowing hard, shaking the windows and whistling sharply down the broad chimney.

Toward midnight, he went to his window and looked out. He had been standing there several minutes when he noticed an unusual light in the Congregational church. John Procter had a study room in the church, but he seldom used it at night. The dean stood watching the gleam through the windows of the vestry. It grew stronger. Suddenly, a sharp tongue of flame shot through the window of one of the doors, and the dean knew at once what the light was.

He ran into the other room and called out to his wife, "The Congregational church is on fire!" He snatched his hat and ran out.

By the time he had reached the church, flames were leaping out of the little windows above the bell in the steeple. Almost the entire town turned out. With the help of the fire department, they saved the parsonage, but the church was completely destroyed. The people drew back in awe as the steeple fell upon the roof, blown by the gale that seemed to drive the tall, blazing torch through the air like a giant spear down through the timbers.

John and Kate Procter, along with Jane, stood in the parsonage yard looking at the smoldering heap. A group of neighbors and church members stood near the minister's family.

The dean approached them. He had been working hard, with scores of other men, carrying John's books out when it looked as if the parsonage might go with the church. He had helped to carry them back again when the danger was over. Several times during the excitement, he had noticed Mr. Harris, the Baptist minister, hard at work. Once, they had hold of the same box containing some valuable papers and pictures from John's library.

"Well," John was saying to one of his parishioners, "this is one less church building in Markham, at any rate."

"I'm very sorry for you, neighbor," said the dean. He was disheveled and dirty, blackened by ashes. His coat was torn across the back, and his whole appearance was very unministerial.

"I'm sincerely grateful for your help, Dean Randall," said John, shaking hands with him heartily. "I won't say that I would like to do the same thing for you sometime, but I certainly owe you much and appreciate your kindness."

"You won't have any place to preach next Sunday," said Mr. Harris, before the dean could reply. "We shall be glad to offer your people the use of the Baptist church in the morning."

John was astonished, as he remembered the list of pastors he had made in his study, and the judgments he'd made about

Harris. He said to himself, *I have done Harris an injustice.*

Then he said aloud, "Thank you very much, Mr. Harris. I accept your offer for my people, with pleasure."

The dean hesitated. It was on his lips to say, "We shall be glad to give your people the use of the cathedral in the evening, neighbor." But he checked himself with the thought of the astonishment that would come into all those faces at such an invitation.

He had taken a step toward John Procter. But just as soon he stepped back, and after another strange hesitation he walked away.

---

When Dean Randall got home, he lay down on his lounge in the study. It was nearly morning. His wife thought he was asleep. He was wide awake and asking himself the question, *Shall I invite Procter to use my pulpit next Sunday or the Sunday after?* But when the morning finally dawned, the question had still not found an answer.

# 5.
# The Power of Christian Community

❦

T WAS EARLY ON THE SUNDAY morning after the Congregational church had burned down. John Procter was in his study reading over the sermon that he expected to preach in the Baptist church.

He had chosen a sermon he had preached to his own people several years before—one of his best, so his wife said. There was nothing in it that could possibly offend anyone of another denomination. *It is a sermon just as good for one person as for another*, John said to himself as he walked up and down, studying his manuscript.

It was nearly half past ten when Jane knocked at the door and handed him a note.

"The servant brought it over just now from the dean," she said. "She is waiting for an answer."

The dean had never written him a letter, and he had no possible hint as to what the note contained. It was, therefore, with the greatest astonishment that John Procter read the following:

> My Dear Brother and Neighbor,
>
> I understand that Brother Cameron of the Presbyterian church has invited you to speak from his pulpit this evening, but will you accept my invitation to occupy the pulpit of Grace Cathedral next Sunday morning? If you will reply by a word and send it over by the servant, I will announce to my people at my service this morning, and Brother Harris can do the same from his pulpit. Mrs. Randall joins me in sympathy with you for your loss, and congratulates Mrs. Procter and yourself on the saving of your parsonage.
>
> In Christ's name,
> Nathan Randall

If the dean had come into his study and handed him baskets full of money, John could hardly have been more astonished than he was by this note. He read the note again. There was no mistake about it. The dean had actually invited him to preach in the Episcopal church. It was an unheard-of thing. It had never happened in Markham before. But even in the midst of his astonishment and excitement, John said to himself, *I don't know why I ought to be so surprised. If we are all Christians, why not?* He stood a moment with the note in his hand. Then he remembered that the servant was waiting. He stepped out into the hall. Kate and Jane were ready for church and waiting for him.

"Are you ready, John?" Kate said. "It's time to go."

John told her of the note he'd received.

She said immediately, "There's only one answer to give to such an invitation. Tell him yes."

John looked at his wife and daughter and then stepped back into his study and wrote his reply. It was very short, but he experienced more emotion while writing it than he felt over most of his sermons.

> My Dear Brother, Dean Randall—
>
> I am glad to accept your invitation to preach next Sunday morning in Grace Cathedral. I accept it in the same spirit of Christian fellowship that prompted you to make it. We thank you for your sympathy and pray for great blessings on you and your people today.
>
> Your neighbor,
>
> John Procter

As John walked with his wife and daughter toward the Baptist church, Kate said, "Were you ever more surprised in your life?"

"No, I don't know as I ever was," John replied.

Jane added, "Mrs. Randall told me that Francis—her son out in Pyramid—recently invited the Congregational minister there to preach in his pulpit."

"Seems as if the father is following his son's example," said Kate with a slight smile.

"It's very remarkable," John said. His mind was excited by the event, but he was silent until they reached the church. Kate and Jane went in, and he went around to the side entrance where the minister's study was.

The church was filled to overflowing. John's congregation turned out almost to a member, and the Baptist people were present more largely than usual. Nearly every person in the audience was known to John personally, and all of them sympathized with him in his loss. During his fifteen years' residence in Markham, he had won the respect and confidence of his townsmen, and they all liked him as a preacher.

The first distinct surprise to the congregation came when the Baptist minister gave several announcements. He mentioned many items relating to his own church, including the preaching of John Procter at the Presbyterian church in the evening, and then after a little pause he said, "I must also announce, especially for the benefit of our friends from the Congregational church who are with us today, that their pastor, by invitation from Dean Randall, will preach in Grace Cathedral next Sunday morning."

A distinct shock went over the people. They turned and looked questioningly at one another. Many whispered to their neighbors, "What was that? Did he say the Episcopal church?"

The second memorable feature of the service was John's sermon. When he rose and laid his manuscript on the open Bible, he was seen to hesitate a moment, and then slowly closed the Bible and his written sermon within it.

He stood a moment looking over the pulpit to the people, and then began to talk about the fire that had destroyed his church. He could not let the occasion go by, he said, without thanking his townsmen for the prompt assistance they had given him and his family during the danger threatening his home. He felt as if he owed a special word of thanksgiving to his neighbor, the pastor of the church where he and his people were grateful guests this morning, for the careful zeal he had shown in looking after the books and pictures in his study at the parsonage.

All this the people listened to with pleased interest, and it seemed entirely in keeping with the character of the occasion. But they were evidently waiting and expecting the minister to open the Bible and begin his sermon. Instead of doing so, John went on with a natural continuation of his personal remarks about the helpfulness shown on the night of the fire, to speak in general about the power that an entire Christian community might have if it would unite as one to save the whole town from the common danger of sin as it had united to save his family.

"There is the fire of alcohol consumption, for example," John Procter went on, and he had never preached better. "It is a fire that threatens every home one way or another. What a fight we could make against it if all the Christians in Markham were united. There is the fire of greed, which causes some people to amass riches while others go hungry. If the Christian people in all the churches really came together as one, could they not put that fire out? There is the fire of vice and crime, which grow worse each year. Is not that a common danger that we ought to be facing together? There is the fire of corrupt selfish political control of our own town. If all the church members in Markham always voted together for the best man regardless of national party divisions, could we not elect the men of our choice and put out forever this fire of personal selfishness that burns within the state and endangers all the best life of our community? If we were working together with a common purpose as disciples of one Master, do you not think we could prevail?"

Heads nodded in assent all over the sanctuary. Surely, if they would all turn out in a body, as they had done to save one another's property from physical fire, it was beyond a doubt more necessary still to unite to put out these other fires that endangered the souls of the people. Corruption and crime were growing worse in the town each year. Standards of morality were lowering more and more each year. Meanwhile, Markham had twelve churches, twelve ministers, twelve church buildings, prayer meetings, preaching, and all the forms of religious life. But it was not directed toward a common end, to further the kingdom of God in Markham.

Throughout his sermon, John was careful not to mention—or even hint at—denominational differences. He spoke of *one body* of believers. He finished his sermon with such a loving and Christian spirit that all were touched by it. He alluded, in words of gratitude, to the brotherly spirit that had prompted the Baptist people to welcome his own that morning. He spoke of the service that had been announced for the Episcopal church the next Sunday with a deep feeling for such a union of Christian believers. And he concluded the sermon with a prayer of unusual power and beauty that the Holy Spirit might lead them into all the truth and make possible the loving prayer of

Jesus that His disciples might be one, even as He was one with the Father.

Later, Charles Harris and John Procter walked slowly away from the church, together. They were the last to leave.

"I want to thank you again for that sermon," said Mr. Harris, when he reached the corner where he was to turn down another street to his home.

"I am very glad if I spoke right, if I in any way helped them see the need for unity," John replied.

"I believe you did," said Harris. He paused and then, looking at John, said, "I suppose you and I really, deep down, want to see God's will done in Markham. But I suppose we have either purposely or ignorantly misunderstood each other. Don't you think perhaps all of us ministers here in Markham have failed to know each other as we might?"

John was startled. Again he recalled his own critical description of the different ministers of Markham as he thought he knew them.

"I have no doubt of it," he replied. "We criticize and condemn without knowing the facts, without really knowing one another. But if we only could get together—"

"Perhaps we shall sometime," the Baptist minister said.

The two men paused for a moment, looking into each other's faces with a new and kinder look than they had ever known. They parted with a friendly handshake, and each walked home very thoughtfully.

That evening, John spoke again on the same theme in the Presbyterian church. He was at first tempted to take his written sermon that he had expected to use in the morning. But the glow of the morning service had grown into a white heat that reflected the passion of the man. John's passion spread among the people in the Presbyterian church, and his words clearly touched the hearts of many people.

Hugh Cameron thanked John Procter with tears in his eyes.

"We must have you and your people with us again soon," he said heartily, as they parted at the close of the service, and again the two ministers felt the thrill of an unaccustomed fellowship in the clasp of hands.

That night, it seemed the churches might be led out of their long years of sectarian habits. And yet John still wrestled with the old questions: *How can the churches ever really unite? Can it be done without a miracle? The emotions are easy to stir. Is it any more that has been done today?*

Nevertheless, he went forward that week with a new sensation as he anticipated the service in the Episcopal church. What should he preach about? Would it be wise to continue this same subject of church unity? He had never given so much thought to the subject of a sermon since he left the seminary twenty-five years before.

6.

# An Interview with the Bishop

❦

S DEEPLY AS THE TWO congregations had been moved that Sunday by John Procter's preaching, it was insignificant compared with the invitation to preach in Grace Cathedral the following week. Before the end of the week, the news had reached the ears of Bishop Park, who lived only twenty-five miles from Markham. Dean Randall's church was in his diocese, and the two men were friends. In fact, Dean Randall was quite assured of Park's support in the coming selection of a new bishop.

The dean was in his study Friday morning when the servant announced Bishop Park's unexpected arrival. There was a moment of confusion on the dean's face as his mentor entered the room, but he quickly recovered himself. Without a word, he quietly waited for the bishop to begin the conversation.

The bishop was a large man with an unusually good-natured, easygoing temperament. He was exceedingly popular with the clergy of his diocese. His friendship with Dean Randall dated from college days.

"I suppose you know why I have come over this morning," Bishop Park said. Though he was smiling and genial as always, he seemed a bit uncomfortable.

"I imagine you have heard of my invitation to John Procter." The dean pointed to his desk and a letter lying there. "I was just writing to you about it."

"I do not need to tell you it is a most astonishing piece of news," Bishop Park said. "In fact, it is so remarkable that I have come to verify it from your own lips. It is the last thing I ever expected from you."

"It is the last thing I ever expected of myself," the dean replied with a voice and manner that betrayed his inner struggle.

"Of course," continued the bishop with just a faint trace of irritation in his tone. "Yet you know that in giving this invitation to a minister of another denomination, you are violating one of the canons of the church. I do not need to remind so old a churchman as you are of this." The bishop said it with the nearest approach to sarcasm he was ever known to use.

"Of course, that goes without saying," the dean answered quietly.

"In asking him to perform one of the functions of our church, the preaching of the Word, you violate one of our distinct and absolute laws. You throw the established order into confusion, and in doing so, you overthrow your own priestly order. In short, my friend, your action in this matter is entirely lawless and will lead to grave consequences, I fear. I am absolutely astonished when I think of you, of all men, acting so irresponsibly."

The color drained from Dean Randall's face as he listened. He took a deep breath before he replied, "I realize the truth of all you have said. I have traveled the same ground as you. But—" The dean looked straight at Bishop Park. "But as man to man, Christian to Christian, may there not come a time when the laws of his church are of less authority to a man than a higher law which God bids him follow? Are the laws of my church more binding on me than the laws of my conscience or my sense of what is Christlike?"

The bishop did not reply immediately. His usually easy countenance was now clouded with deep thought.

Finally, he said, "I don't deny that in many ways some of the canons of the Episcopal church have become obsolete, no longer anything but traditions. But to allow church functions to be performed by other ministers is to cause a serious break in the established order of our church life."

"But can you tell me," Dean Randall said, "what possible harm can come to anyone if a good Christian man, of great usefulness as a minister, a man of long experience in the church, preaches the gospel standing in the pulpit of Grace Cathedral? He is as much a Christian disciple as you or I. He believes in the same teaching and practices it in his daily life. He is going to the same heaven. What possible harm can come from his preaching in my church?"

Again, the bishop showed signs of temper. He rose and spoke more forcefully. "That is not the question at all. The question is purely one of our church canon. It is simply a question of whether you, an Episcopal clergyman, deliberately choose to make a law for yourself in defiance of the one which the church has laid down for you to follow. I do not question the Christian character of Mr. Procter. From all I know of him, he is a most worthy man. But if you invite him to preach in Grace Cathedral, you deliberately trespass on one of the established orders of the Episcopal church. You cease to be a representative of that church. And you make yourself an example of lawless conduct in the church, which will create confusion and trouble."

The dean was silent. A great crisis had suddenly and unexpectedly come upon him, and he knew his own ambitions might be compromised if he made the slightest misstep.

Noticing the dean's hesitation, Bishop Park went on. "Be guided by me in this matter. You can, with gentleness, rescind this hasty invitation. It may be true that people will not understand your change of mind, but the outside world does not understand the action of the Episcopal church in this matter anyway."

"I cannot go back now," replied the dean in a low voice. "I have given the invitation to Brother Procter, and he has accepted it in good faith. I feel that it is right and in keeping with Christ's desire that His disciples become as one."

The bishop was silent for a long time after the dean had

finished. Then he said, speaking with a forcefulness that the dean could not help but notice, "Of course, Randall, all this, you know well enough, makes any possible opportunity for you to receive the choice for the bishop's office out of the question. No man can expect to fill that place who deliberately disobeys a definite canon of the church."

"Of course," replied the dean. "I have thought that out."

In all his experience, the bishop had never had a similar case. The dean's prominence in the church, his scholarly reputation, his standing as a churchman, were sure to make his actions remarkable. It was a case that could not be overlooked. What the final result would be, not even the bishop was prepared to say.

---

The same day of the bishop's visit, the trustees of the Congregational church held an important meeting. It was to be a regular monthly business meeting, but every other matter was overshadowed by the burning of the church building and the subject of rebuilding.

"It's a very hard time, just now, to raise money," said Deacon Bruce, with a sigh. "Crops have failed and business is slow."

"That's so," added Mr. Rose, the chairman of the board. "Of course, our insurance will help us some, but it is not enough to put up such a building as we ought to have."

"If we build again, we ought to build of stone, instead of wood, it seems to me," remarked another member of the board.

"The Sunday school rooms ought to be made more modern," said the superintendent. "I realize that will mean even more money, but we must think toward the future."

The church treasurer, who had been busily scribbling numbers on a sheet of paper, gave a low whistle. "Rebuilding a church is an enormous undertaking—and extremely costly. I don't know where we'll come up with so much money."

John Procter had said little so far. He had replied to questions, but had not ventured to make any remarks about the cost of a new building, or its size, or architecture.

"I would like to ask our pastor what he thinks about the building project," the chairman said. "Give us your thoughts, John."

All the faces turned toward the pastor. For fifteen years, the church officers had consulted him repeatedly in matters that belonged to the business affairs of the parish, and his judgment and good sense had always been highly prized.

He looked around the little group of churchpeople. He was grave and thoughtful.

"The fact is, dear friends, that I have reached a conclusion in regard to a new church building that will, perhaps, astonish you. I have come to believe that it would be best for us not to rebuild at all, because there are too many church buildings in Markham already."

The entire group of church officers was bewildered into silence. They looked at John Procter with questioning expressions.

At last the chairman of the board managed to stammer, “Why, what, how do you mean, John? What can we do as a church if we have no building?”

“We can worship and work with some other church in Markham,” replied John calmly.

The hush of silence that fell over the room was the first sign of a wonderful revolution in the established church life of Markham.

7.

# William Hears a Sermon

HEN WILLIAM PROCTER walked into the Episcopal church of Pyramid the Sunday following his meeting with Francis Randall, he was prepared to criticize, in detail, everything he saw and heard.

The spirit of dissatisfaction in him that had compelled him to leave the seminary and give up the ministry had never been so strong. William was in a mood that marks and magnifies trifles. He found himself sneering just a little at the robe Randall wore when he appeared in the chancel. He was tempted to criticize the singing of the choir, some of whom were obviously unfamiliar with the music of the service. He thought the rituals and liturgies were nothing but hollow formalities.

But gradually the spirit of the man in the pulpit began to change William's mind. There was no hollow formality in the way Francis read the prayers, which were quite beautiful. He was compelled to acknowledge that Francis read them uncommonly well and with passion. As he followed the words silently, calling them up in memory, William wondered if he himself could have put as much feeling into the same sentences every Sunday morning the year around.

So it came about that when it came time for the sermon, William had passed into a spirit of ready acceptance of the truth, and his critical, dissatisfied mind was ready to receive anything the preacher had to give that was worthwhile.

The sermon was quite practical. It was simply a call to the Christian men and women of Pyramid to do something to remove the gambling saloons that filled the town with crime and disorder. There was nothing old-fashioned or formal in the way Francis called attention to the need of a better town. He spoke with deep conviction and seemed at times to be on the verge of tears. There were two sentences in the sermon near the close that struck William's mind with great force.

"Any Christian living in Pyramid today is a coward and is faithless if he does not do all in his power to confront this gambling curse," Francis said. "No one has any right to say it is none of his business."

William slipped out of the church service and went to his little room in the boardinghouse near the mill. The sermon was not at all what he had expected. He had imagined he might hear some kind of a churchly discourse on one of the Jewish sinners of the Old Testament with two or three moral lessons to be drawn from their evil behavior. But this uncompromising call to Christian duty was unexpected. It aroused in William a sense of duty that was too deep in him to be easily turned aside.

What had he done? It is true he had conscientiously left the ministry because he could not honestly preach in a pulpit. But had he also abandoned his responsibility for the salvation of the world? What business was it of his that gambling halls in Pyramid cursed the young men of the place? Could he leave his work in the mill to fight such an evil? It was a part of all mining camps and an evil that could not be attacked without great personal danger. Why did Randall want to get tangled in any such thankless reform business? Why couldn't he go on and preach in a general way against sin, and let this particular sin alone? He had not been so stirred up over anything since he had written that letter to his father while still in seminary.

When he entered the mill the next morning, he was unable to shake off the burden of responsibility that the sermon had laid upon him. In a spirit of mingled anger and self-reproach, he went about his duties in the mill. Not even the roar and rattle and heat of the grim mixer, as it entered the white-hot furnace where the ore was burning, was able to drown the voice of religious conviction for the sin of others that now burned white hot in his soul.

---

The Sunday morning in Markham that followed the events of that week, John Procter was to preach in Dean Randall's pulpit, and it must be said that many of the members of the other churches deserted their own services to go to the Episcopal church.

A great many rumors had agitated the town of Markham during the week. It was said that the bishop had been to see

Dean Randall about the matter of his invitation to John Procter and that strong words had passed between them. It was even whispered by some that the two men had almost come to blows and that the dean's unheard-of action would not pass unchallenged by the church leadership.

In addition to all this, rumors of the meeting held Friday night by the officers of John Procter's church caused even more excitement. It was said by some that he had advised his board of trustees to disband the Congregational church altogether and unite with the Baptists. Others said the meeting Friday night had ended in a sharp quarrel between the pastor and his church officers, and that he had immediately tendered his resignation. It was definitely known beyond any question that a meeting of the entire congregation had been called for the following Monday night, and at that time some very interesting and unusual affairs would be discussed. The meeting, through the courtesy of the Presbyterians, was to be held in their church.

It was, therefore, with an unparalleled interest that the service began that morning in Grace Cathedral. The building was not large, and it was as crowded as if a fashionable wedding were taking place in it. Some people had to stand during the entire service. The little vestibule was packed with people looking over one another's shoulders and standing on tiptoe trying to see, while many from the other churches, who came a little late, were unable to find even standing room. Instead of going to their own churches, most of these people stood about the little yard in front of Grace Cathedral, discussing the events of the week.

It is safe to say that when John Procter at last rose to preach, he had the full attention of the assembled congregation. His subject, which he announced at once, was, "What Would Jesus Do if He Were a Member of a Church Today?"

The answer to this question revealed to everyone present some simple truths. Surely, the pastor said, Jesus would seek to eliminate division among churches and encourage unity. Genuine love and unselfish service among believers would attract the attention of all community members. The application was direct and largely left to the people to make for themselves. As John went on, the impression deepened. Even the people standing in the vestibule farthest from the speaker felt the truth of the message.

At the close of the service, people remained seated and silent longer than usual. It seemed to the two ministers as they went into the little room by the chancel where the dean took off his robe that a baptism like that of the Holy Spirit at Pentecost had fallen on the people.

8.

# John Procter's Proposal

HAT WAS A BEAUTIFUL MESSAGE you brought to us," said the dean as he faced John in the little room.

John looked at the dean thoughtfully. "I was very eager to give the people something helpful."

"You did. And it helped me." The dean spoke plainly but in a tone that moved John Procter deeply.

"I do not need to say that this morning's experience has been, in many ways, the most remarkable I have ever known in my ministry," said John. "I am sure you know very well how deeply I feel the fellowship you have extended to me. Although—" he continued with a little hesitation "—I do not know all it may cost you."

"I'm sure it will cost me something, but that is a small matter compared to the good that might come of this," said the dean. Then he added, "You are passing through a new experience in your own church. Are you really not going to build again?"

"I shall advise my people not to build, but to unite with one of the other churches," John replied. "When the time comes, I want your advice and counsel."

"You shall have it, gladly," the dean said.

They were about to exit out of the side door, when John Procter said, "Neighbor, shall we pray together before we go?"

For several years, Dean Randall had not prayed aloud any prayers except those printed in the Prayer Book. Now he knelt down beside his neighbor, and John prayed simply but tenderly for a blessing on all the churches in Markham, that they might truly fulfill Christ's desire for them to be one. When he had finished, there was a curious silence for a moment before the dean uttered a word. To his own astonishment, the dean found the act full of newness and power. Never before had he joined with a minister of another denomination in a common prayer for a common blessing upon the work of Christ.

---

On Monday night, the members of the Congregational Church of Markham met in the Presbyterian church to discuss the subject of rebuilding. Nearly the entire membership was present. John opened the meeting by asking for the chairman's report.

"We met," Mr. Rose said, "to discuss the subject of rebuilding. We talked over plans and expense. There was some difference of opinion on the part of the trustees and church officers as to the kind of building we ought to put up. Almost all of us agreed that it's an unusually hard time just now to raise money. But there was no doubt in the mind or speech of any of us as to the necessity of building some kind of a church—that is, until our pastor was asked to give his advice. What he said then was so unexpected, and we were so little prepared to entertain his view, that after a discussion that resulted in nothing more satisfactory, it was voted by the board to lay the whole matter before the entire church and have it discussed by the membership. The pastor's proposition is now known to you. I would, of course, much prefer to have him explain to the church what he said to us Friday night."

The chairman, after a moment of hesitation, sat down, and everyone looked intently at John. For fifteen years, the members of the Congregational Church of Markham had trusted and respected him, and while they were astonished beyond measure at what they had heard of the meeting Friday night, they were still ready to listen to their pastor in explanation of his strange plan.

He rose and looked at his people thoughtfully before he said anything. The occasion marked a crisis for him and them.

At last, he said, "What I said to the board Friday night was this: I do not think we ought to rebuild our church. Instead of doing that, we can better work and worship with some other church in Markham. Of course, I do not expect such a proposal to be accepted by the church at once, or without grave and serious consideration. You deserve to hear my reasons for such advice."

There was much stirring and murmuring among the church members, and John waited a moment before continuing.

"There are already twelve churches and twelve ministers in Markham," he explained. "The population of the town gives less than two hundred people to each church. Our own membership is one hundred and twenty. The Presbyterians here have a membership of about the same. None of the other churches in the town has over one hundred members. Nearly every church in town is burdened with a debt, and many can barely afford to pay their pastor a decent wage."

He paused to let all that sink in, and then proceeded. "Brethren, those are the plain facts about the churches in Markham, as I stated them to the board Friday night during our discussion. Now, will you let me try to show, in a concise way, what advantages will be found for us and for the town by uniting with one of the other churches already organized in Markham. I have put in writing, for the sake of exactness, a number of points that contain my own convictions."

The pastor then read his reasons for believing that both the town and its churches would be better served if their congregations united with another already in existence. He pleaded his case that the churches of Markham already struggled with debt and small memberships, while the moral fiber of the town suffered. He ended by saying, "Instead of being the death of our church, this move could be the beginning of the best life it has ever felt."

When John finished reading from his paper, the silence remained unbroken. The members of the Congregational church were not able to say anything for a long time. Nothing like this had ever happened before. No such proposition had ever been put before them. They were bewildered by it. There were some of the older members, however, who had followed the pastor's reading with sober and even angry opposition. One of these, Roland Walker, was the first to break the silence.

"Mr. Procter," Roland said in a voice full of emotion, "your astonishing plan did not explain what you propose to do with the pastor of the church, or what you propose the church to do with him. If our church unites with another, one of them will have to give up its minister. If we were to unite with the Presbyterians, for example, do you suppose their minister would be willing to step down or his people be willing to have his place filled by another man? There are too many practical business difficulties in what you propose."

Roland sat down, and again the churchpeople all turned eagerly toward the pastor.

"I have believed for a long time," he said, after a moment, "that there were too many churches in Markham. But I do not believe there are too many ministers. Brother Walker, how many men are there employed in the bank where you are now?"

"Four," replied Roland. "There is a cashier, a teller, a bookkeeper, and a janitor."

"Four men on salary to do the necessary business of the bank," John said. "There is not a grocery store in Markham that does not employ at least one clerk to take orders and deliver goods. There is not a general merchandise store that does not have at least two or three paid helpers. Now, as matters are at present, it is true that there are twice as many church buildings and organizations as Markham needs. But it is not oversupplied with Christian men to do the necessary Christian work."

Noticing some quizzical expressions, John decided to elaborate. "What I mean is that if we could reduce the number of churches in Markham to six, we would still have use for twelve ministers. That would not be at all out of proportion to the need of religious work to be done. If we should unite with the Presbyterians, there will still be enough for both Brother Cameron and myself to do. No minister with a church membership of two hundred people in a community like ours ever can do alone all that ought to be done. I am of the opinion that in time the churches will all employ more men to do their work. No other business is ever done in the world as the churches do theirs. If the work of a bank requires four men, it generally has four men. But the pastor of a church is supposed to take care of all its business alone no matter how fast it grows or its needs increase. There will be no trouble about having two ministers in the church if only the church realizes the value of the work to be done for this town."

Again, there was a long silence in the room.

John Procter spoke again. "I know, of course, that what I have proposed is so strange to many of you that you are not prepared to take any action on it at this meeting. But strange and even impossible as it may seem to you at first, I still hope you will take time to consider it."

"We certainly cannot act on this at once," said one of the deacons, an elderly man who had been a member of the

Congregational church for more than forty years. He was going on to express his opinion as to the wisdom of such a remarkable movement, and several others were evidently now ready to say something, when someone down near the door came forward with a note for John.

It was marked, "Urgent."

"The boy is at the door and will take your answer," said the man who had come up to the pulpit with the message.

The deacon paused a moment until the interruption at the platform was over.

John opened the envelope and read the message. It was from Pyramid and dated late that evening. It read:

> Rev. John Procter, Markham:
>
> William has met with very serious accident in mill.
>
> Come at once.
>
> Francis Randall

John read this over twice before he fully realized what it meant. He rose, pale and shaken, and told his people what the news was.

"I shall have time to leave for the west on the midnight express," he said. As he passed down through the aisle of the church to hurry home with the news, more than one hand was thrust out to express sympathy. It had all happened so unexpectedly that the congregation remained in a convulsion of uncertainty when the door closed on their pastor.

The deacon spoke. He had been one of the first to wish John and his son well as he hurried down the aisle. "We can't settle this question of church building tonight.

We need to think it over carefully. I move that we spend the rest of the time in prayer for the pastor and his family."

The deacon's motion was carried, and the church, stirred by a sympathy that grew out of genuine affection for their pastor, offered many earnest prayers for him and all those who were dear to him.

9·

# At Work in the Mill

❦

INCE HEARING FRANCIS Randall's remarkable sermon, William Procter had not attended any church. He had not yet settled the question of his own responsibility as a Christian.

He kept saying to himself that he had not come out to Pyramid to do the work of a missionary or a reformer. At the same time, he knew well enough that he was like hundreds of other men who, when they move west, find it easy to shirk religious duties and take a holiday from all Christian work. Often this holiday lasts the rest of a man's life.

William went to his mill duties every morning discontented and restless, half angry at Randall. He was not suited to the life of labor he now lived. In addition was his memory of those days in Andover when the woman he loved rejected him because he would not continue in the ministry. With bitterness he fought the feelings he still had for her.

He had tried to forget, but his efforts had been useless. Memory was stronger and more tenacious than oblivion.

So he went about his work in the mill, a strange mixture of human passions and struggles in the midst of weird and clashing monsters of iron and steel and poisonous vats and tanks of chemicals.

There was a twelve-inch board across the top of one of the large cyanide vats over which the men in the mill often walked to reach another part of the building. It saved a journey around by way of a pair of steps and a ladder, and the men were in the habit of crossing by means of this plank, although they knew well enough that a slip and a plunge into the poisonous fluid would mean death. They had become so used to it that in their rough way they often calculated on the length of time a man might survive if he fell into the vat, even supposing he was a good swimmer and help was not far off.

That morning, as he crossed this narrow plank, William had a curious feeling that an easy accident would put an end to all his mental troubles. There was only a twelve-inch plank between life and death. He quickly ran across the plank and sat down trembling at the foot of the vat. He did not cross the board again that day.

He had come into the mill at ten o'clock. The mill was running night and day to fill orders, and everything in it, including the men, was taxed to its fullest capacity. Between six and seven o'clock that evening, William was called into the furnace room to help one of the men who was repairing a part of the track on which the two mixers continually traveled on their circular way.

The work of the mill was too valuable to be stopped, so the repairing went on while the red-hot mixer plunged into its fiery bath with a clanging of metal doors that closed behind it to protect the fires and emerged again with the same crash of iron on iron. Then the carriage, white hot from its invisible and awful journey through the blast, broke out of its prison and flung itself around the circle of steel rails, withering everything with its intense heat and, as evening came on, filling the narrow room with a light that glowed remorselessly from its blades and arms.

Often, to William, standing fascinated in the presence of this strange metal monster, pressing back against the walls of the mill to keep from being hit, it seemed that the thing was alive and conscious, and waiting only for its time to fling itself off the track and strike him down with its murderous white-hot fists for pleasure.

He crawled under the track where the other man was trying to screw a bolt into a part of the iron foundation on which the track rested. When the mixer passed over them, it seemed to William as if the heat would suffocate him. He wondered at the workers who moved about for hours in the unnatural heat and labored in such places as this.

The two men worked hard, panting with the heat and scorched with the fine particles of ore dust that fell from the mixers as they crossed the track in turn above them. But after working several minutes, they were not able to screw the bolt into its place.

"You will have to go into the toolhouse and get the large wrenches," William said to his companion. He could have gone himself, but he felt some compassion for the man who had been at work longer than usual in his cramped position. The man crawled out from under the track, and William was left alone. He waited until the heat became so unbearable that he finally crept out and went over at the side of the furnace room to wait for the man to come back.

It is not clear how it happened, for no one was in the furnace room on that side at the time. It seemed probable from William's own disconnected account afterward that he had started to go from the place where he first stood to one of the doors. He was probably absentminded, thinking over his troubles. In the dusk, lighted by the glow of the two mixers as they alternately burst from the furnace, a terrible thing happened. The machine at last had met its opportunity. One of the long metal arms above the stirring blades caught the sleeve of William's shirt as he walked along.

He came to himself in an instant and, realizing his great danger, reached out his other hand to loosen his sleeve. It was burning, but the long, pointed piece of metal had been thrust through the tough cloth and he was unable to pull his arm loose at once. He could feel the red-hot iron burning into the flesh, but he still kept calm, as he walked along by the machine and strained with all his might. He probably would have succeeded in breaking away, but just then his foot struck the tool the man had dropped on the floor when he went out.

He stumbled and fell forward. In doing so, he tore his arm away from the mixer but fell behind it full upon the circular track, striking his head as he fell. He lay unconscious in the path of the other mixer, which had just entered the furnace. The time between the two mixers was about twenty-five seconds. The furnace room was still empty. The workman had not returned.

The second machine rumbled out of the furnace and rolled down, grim and terrible, toward its victim. Still the room was empty, except for William lying across the track. One hand feebly moved. The head stirred a little. A breath of the cool evening from the hills blew into the open door and even gained a little into the blast of the heat over the track. But William Procter still lay there, and the mixer almost upon him, when a man stepped through the open door and looked into the mill.

In the triumphant glow of the advancing machine, he saw the form of the man on the track. With a cry, he leaped up astride the track, lifted up the body, and leaped down again with it. As he did so, one of the mixing blades swept its red-hot side against his hand, burning the whole back of it to a blister.

He staggered with his burden to the open door and laid the man down quietly, resting William's head upon the doorsill. Then he shouted for help. Men came running across the yard and through the furnace room.

The man who had saved William's life looked up as he knelt by the side of the unconscious body. "Bring some water!" he yelled. "Run for the doctor!"

Two men ran in obedience to these orders.

When the doctor came, William was just regaining his senses. The first face he saw was Francis Randall's.

"What's the matter?" he asked feebly.

"You're hurt a little, but the doctor's here. We are going to take you home," said Randall, gently.

William fainted again. The men retrieved a stretcher and carried him over to his boardinghouse, the doctor going along with Randall.

"Is he badly hurt, Doctor?" asked Randall, as he walked along in the dusk, behind the little procession. He wrapped his handkerchief about his hand.

"His right arm is burned to the bone," the doctor said solemnly. "And that burn on his face is a deep one. He must have fallen full force upon the mixer. Did you see the accident? How did it happen?"

"I found him lying unconscious across the track," answered Randall.

"Did you?" asked the doctor, peering curiously at Randall through the dusk.

"Yes," replied Randall. The doctor waited to hear more, but Randall was silent.

"You must have carried him from the track to the door," said the doctor, after a pause.

"Yes. He's not very heavy," replied Randall.

"Humph!" grunted the doctor. But he was used to accidents of all sorts and asked no more questions.

The doctor was busy with William for over an hour. Francis stayed in the room, to be of help, if it was needed. Once, he went out and asked the woman who kept the house to give him some flour to put on his hand. When he came back, the doctor noticed the bandage for the first time.

"You're hurt too, Mr. Randall?"

"A little. I burned my hand."

"Let me see it," said the doctor a little roughly.

Randall hesitated at first, and then smiling wryly, uncovered the wound.

The doctor looked at the wound and then at the clergyman, but said nothing. Randall replaced the covering.

"How is he?" he asked, looking toward the motionless form on the bed.

"To tell the truth, he is in bad shape," the doctor said. "If he has any relatives or friends who ought to be sent for, the quicker the better."

"I know his family," said Randall, sadly. "I'll relay a message right away."

"You'd better. I think the chances are against him. He is badly hurt in the head. If he were my boy, I should want to see him as soon as possible."

So that is how it came about that Francis Randall ran down the hill to the railroad station, and the message was sent flying over the states to Rev. John Procter of Markham who hurried home and broke the news to his wife and Jane.

---

Kate looked at her husband and instantly said, "We will both go to him."

Jane cried to go also, but finally agreed with them that it would not be best. Her mother could do all that was necessary.

As they were packing, Kate suddenly asked her husband, "How did it happen that Francis Randall sent the message?"

"I don't know any more about it than you do," John said. "It was signed by him. That's all I know."

"It's strange," she told him. "Mrs. Randall showed me one of his last letters from Pyramid. He wrote of meeting William, but said that Will was shy and he would not intrude on him. So I had supposed the two seldom met."

"We shall learn all about it when we get there." Then he added, "Should the Lord spare our son."

John nearly broke down. When Jane finally kissed them good-bye, she bravely encouraged her father and mother with words of hope, but when they had gone, she turned back into the parsonage and sobbed. The message had been left on the table. She took it up and read it again. Somehow, the sight of Francis Randall's name at the end of the solemn message comforted her. William was already with a friend. That was worth something to her, as she pictured her father and mother speeding west.

---

During the days that followed, Jane suffered more than the others from the suspense and anxiety. There had come a telegram, announcing their arrival and the fact that William was yet alive. A postcard from her father each day simply announced that William was living, but without improvement. Then, at last, came a letter from her mother that made her heart beat with a variety of emotions. Along with the letter were two copies of the Pyramid daily paper. She read:

> Dear Jane,
>
> I write with a glad heart today. Will is out of danger. The crisis in his favor was reached and passed last

night. The Lord has given me strength far beyond my expectation, and while I have lost a great deal of sleep, I am well and happy. The dear boy is terribly worn by his illness, but this morning he recognized your father and me, and sent his love to you.

I cannot tell you what a wonderful help Francis Randall has been to us during all this experience. We did not learn until we had been here a week how much we owed to him for saving Will's life. I have not yet been inside one of the reduction ore mills, but your father, who visited the one where Will was hurt, gave me a very graphic picture of it.

Francis Randall received a dreadful burn on his right hand. The whole back of it was burned to a crisp. The doctor says he will always carry a great scar. It will be a very honorable one, and we will always take him by that hand with a peculiar feeling of respect and esteem.

Your father will start for home tomorrow, as the affairs of the church are so critical as to call for his personal attention. I shall stay and care for Will as long as it is necessary. Mr. and Mrs. Clark, of the Congregational church, have been very kind to us, as well as many of their people. Perhaps Will may return with me. He is not able yet to talk of the future. Much love to you,

Mother

Jane put the letter back into the envelope and picked up a copy of the Pyramid paper. The article on Francis was over a column long. Jane read it with a feeling of satisfaction. She felt proud that the man who loved her was a hero.

*I never thought that a minister could be a hero,* Jane thought. *And I've never thought of Francis as particularly noble or courageous. Maybe I've misjudged him.*

*10.*

# A Message for William's Girl

❦

HE NEXT MORNING, JANE awoke thinking of her brother and the article in the paper relating to the accident. There had been a brief mention about his time at Andover.

How a newspaperman ever found out anything about William's private romance back there was a mystery to Jane. But somehow it had become known, and Jane was suddenly compelled to do something with the newspaper that she might well have hesitated to do if she could have foreseen all the immediate consequences of it.

She had learned from her brother, before he went out to Pyramid, the name of the Andover young woman whose picture had so agitated him while he was unpacking his trunk. Jane, in a moment of almost anger at this young woman, who had helped to spoil her brother's life, decided to send her the copy of the paper containing the vivid account of William's accident.

She was not as sincere and honest as she usually was, for she sent no word of William's recovery. But there was a feeling within her that said, in quite a hard spirit, *Let her suffer a little if she cares any for him. I'm sure she has hurt him deeply enough.*

So there went out of the Markham post office the next morning a copy of the *Pyramid Miner*, addressed to "Miss Rebecca Phillips, Andover, Mass.," with a certain article marked at the bottom with Jane's initials.

---

The evening of the day after Jane had sent this Pyramid paper, Professor Elias Phillips, of Andover Theological Seminary, was sitting in his study working over some manuscript notes on his new book, an exhaustive analysis of the characteristics of the minor prophets. The evening mail had just been brought to the house by one of the Academy boys, and Rebecca had just come in to the study and laid some letters down on the professor's desk.

"Is that all?" asked the professor a little absently, as he glanced over the letters without opening any of them.

"Yes, except a paper for me," answered his daughter.

She took the paper and went with it into the sitting room. The study door was left ajar.

The professor was so much interested in his notes on the minor prophets that he left his letters unopened on his desk.

A few minutes went by silently. Everything in the old mansion seemed peaceful. It was so quiet that the professor's pen scratched noisily over his paper. He was making good progress with the work.

Suddenly, the scholastic quiet of the professor's surroundings was broken by a loud cry in the other room. He started and sat up straight in his chair. The next moment, the study door opened hastily and his daughter came in. She was pale and unusually excited. It was not a characteristic of the Phillips family to become excited over anything.

"Father, read that!" exclaimed Rebecca, holding out the *Pyramid Miner* and pointing at the article Jane had marked.

The professor turned to the article and read it, without a word or look to betray any emotion.

"Well?" he said, looking up at Rebecca.

"Don't you understand, Father?" Rebecca came closer to him and laid a hand on his shoulder. Then she suddenly knelt down by his chair and laid her proud head on her father's arm. "It is William who is hurt. Perhaps he is dead."

The professor understood immediately. The minor prophets were of minor importance to him for the moment by the side of his daughter's experience.

"Ah, I see. I did not realize what it might mean to you. Rebecca—" he put his hand on her head and remembered that this proud young woman, his only daughter, had lost a mother's counsel when she was a little girl. "Rebecca, is it true, then, that you still care for William Procter?"

"Yes." The answer came in a low voice, but there was no mistaking its sincerity.

"And yet you decided you could not share your life—"

"Father," interrupted Rebecca, "you must telegraph to Pyramid and find out what has happened."

"But this paper is dated nearly two weeks back," said the professor. "If he were fatally injured, surely we would know it by this time."

"Let me see," cried Rebecca, and when she saw the date, her heart leaped up with hope. "Still, Father, we do not know for certain. Won't you go down and send a message?"

"Yes, of course, I will." The professor arose, looking a little sorrowfully at his notes on the desk. He put on his hat and opened the door. Something in his daughter's face, as she stood, looking at him, moved him to shut the door again, and come back to her. "Rebecca," he said, as he bent his gray head and kissed her, "your father is not considered an authority in anything except the Old Testament writers, but if you love William Procter ..."

He looked into his daughter's face and did not need to complete his sentence. She answered his look with one he thought he understood.

When he was gone, Rebecca sat down in her father's chair, and several tears from eyes that nearly all Andover people called proud, fell upon the manuscript relating to the minor prophets.

Professor Phillips went as fast as he could walk to the telegraph station and sent off two telegrams.

Jane opened her telegram with some misgiving. She felt some twinges of conscience as she read it:

> Send word if William Procter is recovering. Haste. My expense.
>
> Elias Phillips,
> Andover, Mass.

At first, Jane had a moment of hesitation, almost as if she did not mean to answer the professor's telegram. But she stepped into the telegraph office on her way to school the next morning and sent the following, directing it not to Professor Phillips, but to Rebecca:

> William out of danger. Very ill. Mother is with him.

Jane did not know Rebecca Phillips at all, but she had a hope that the last four words might cause her some remorse or heartache, or something that would result in William's favor.

---

The other message sent by the professor was to Pyramid. He hesitated for a little before directing the address, but finally sent it to "Rev. Francis Randall, Pyramid, Colorado."

He thought, *Randall must know about it, of course. And he is sure to answer.*

The dean and the professor were old friends. Indeed, it was through the professor that Francis had first heard of William at Pyramid.

An answer to this telegram came promptly:

> Prof. Elias Phillips, Andover, Mass.:
> William out of danger. May lose sight in one eye.
> Francis Randall

---

In Pyramid, the coming of that inquiry from Andover had a peculiar effect on the invalid, lying weak and dependent in the little bedroom of the stuffy boardinghouse near the mill. Randall brought the telegram, and without a word, handed it to William. Randall knew nothing whatever of William's romance.

As William raised his eyes from the telegram, the clergyman said innocently, "Very kind of your old seminary professor to telegraph. It's a little strange he is so late about it. Several weeks now since you were hurt."

"Is it?" asked William. He reread the message, and his imagination began to fill in the cold spaces between the words of the telegram. Would the professor have taken even this late interest in him? If so, perhaps it was possible that Rebecca—

He was too weak to carry on his thought, and when the doctor called, he found his patient had a high fever.

"What have you been doing to him?" he growled testily at Francis Randall who had just risen to go as the doctor came in.

"Nothing," Francis replied. "He had a telegram this morning. Or, rather, I had one inquiring about him."

"Let me see it," said the doctor abruptly.

"Umph! Telegraph back that he will get well if folks will leave him alone," said the doctor, who was more gruff than usual that morning.

But William rallied in the afternoon and steadily grew stronger. The more he thought of the telegram, the more hopeful he became that Rebecca still did care for him. When his father had gone back to Markham and his mother was alone with him, he confided his secret to her, and she comforted him as only a mother can.

---

Even during the anxious moments John had spent by his son's bedside, the thoughts of his church in Markham had been with him. That it was at a great crisis in its history he knew very well. How the matter would finally be settled he was unable to declare with any certainty. Would a majority of his members vote to unite with the Presbyterians or some other congregation? If they did, would the minority proceed to form another church and so make matters as bad as they were before? How would the other churches take such a union? Would it make them more jealous than ever because such a union would make the largest, strongest church in Markham?

He was not able to answer these questions. Nevertheless, he was fully committed in his own mind to the principle of union, as he had outlined it to his people.

He got home on Saturday and learned that a meeting of the church had been called for the following Monday in anticipation of his return. When Sunday came, for the first time in nearly fifteen years he found that he was not engaged anywhere to preach. He had returned hurriedly and very many of the people, even in his own parish, did not know that he was back.

John hesitated a little when the hour for service came that morning, and finally decided to go and hear Harris, the Baptist minister. He had often heard him spoken of as narrow-minded and judgmental in certain ways, and he thought he would go and hear for himself.

"Brother Harris happily disappointed me once; perhaps he will again," said John, as Jane and he went along together.

As they went into the church, they noticed and spoke to several of their own churchpeople and friends. When they were seated, they could not help noticing a large number of the Congregational people scattered through the sanctuary.

"Look, Father," whispered Jane, after a moment, as people were still coming in. "It's Communion Sunday here! See the table?"

They were seated only three or four pews from the front on the side aisle. John had noticed the Communion table when he sat down. Jane's whisper simply emphasized a curiously exciting emotion he now began to feel at the sight of the familiar emblems on the table.

*Will Brother Harris be receptive to the sudden appearance of so many from the Congregational church—people who hold some different views from his own? Will he think all these people, including myself, are here to scrutinize him and his way of doing things? And will there be any hesitation in allowing us to partake of the Lord's Supper?* These questions came into John's mind with all the force of a most serious and important event.

The pulpit was still empty. The Rev. Charles Harris had not yet come out of the room behind the platform. The church was nearly full, and the organist was still playing the prelude. John, with a feeling of growing expectancy, sat there with his eyes on the door that led from the pastor's study to his pulpit.

11.

# According to the Master's Commands

❦

CHARLES HARRIS AT LAST opened the door back of the pulpit platform and came out. After a moment, he lifted his head and looked over the congregation.

As his eyes rested on that part of the church where John and Jane were seated, he made a movement as if he intended to go down and speak to him. He had half risen from his seat but seemed to change his mind, for he sat down again, and when he finally did rise it was to open the regular service of the church.

It was the custom in the First Baptist Church of Markham to have a regular preaching service before the Communion. The pastor then came down from the pulpit and stood behind the table. If there were any baptisms, they took place immediately after the sermon. The pastor then stepped back into his room to change from his baptismal dress and came out into the church room through the side door, which opened at the end of one of the side aisles.

There were several baptisms on this special day. Charles Harris went on with the service up to the point of the sermon, appearing a bit nervous. The sermon itself was not remarkable in any way, though sincere. During the baptisms that followed, both John and Jane were impressed with the proceedings. They had never been present at such a service, and they were struck with the simplicity and earnestness of the minister and those who presented themselves for membership.

After the baptisms, there was an unusually long time before the minister appeared. The choir had finished its hymn and sat down. The organist continued playing, but it was evident to John from the actions of people around him that the prolonged absence of the minister was unusual.

At last, when the waiting of the congregation had grown to be painfully awkward, the door that everyone was now looking at opened, and Harris appeared. He came into the church slowly and deliberately shut the door as he faced the people. For an instant, he stood still. Then he walked directly down the aisle to where John was sitting and bent over and whispered something to him.

The church was very quiet, and everyone was looking intently at the two ministers. In the next moment John rose from his seat and followed Charles Harris up to the Communion table. He sat down in the seat where Harris motioned, while the pastor remained standing, facing his people.

The members of First Baptist Church recognized this as an unusual event. There was no law or rule in the church forbidding other denominations from partaking of the Communion. It had simply been a custom dating back to the organization of the church. And never yet had that custom been changed or varied.

Harris spoke slowly, but distinctly. "I have taken the liberty today of inviting Rev. John Procter to the Lord's table to assist me. We shall be glad to have our friends of the Congregational church partake of the emblems with us according to the Master's command."

He looked about for a moment, and then said, "Blessed be the tie that binds our hearts in Christian love."

Then he offered a prayer and served the bread. He asked John to follow him in the service of the cup. All through the congregation, there was a deepening feeling of interest. It reached its climax when, at the close of the Communion, the minister spoke a few words, in which he referred to the sermon preached by John the first Sunday after his own church was burned down.

Later, when the service was over and the people had filed out, Harris said, "Will you come into the study a moment, John?" The two ministers went into the little room back of the pulpit.

"I feel as if some explanation were due you for my action today," began Charles Harris, with the same noticeable nervousness he had shown in the pulpit. This soon passed away as he went on with his explanation. "You see, when I stepped in here after the baptism, I had not made up my mind about inviting you and your people to the Lord's

Supper. I had thought of it the moment I saw you, but I was not sure that I ought to break an old and established custom of our church. When the baptisms were finally over and I had come in here, I had an unusual experience. Since the burning of your church and your preaching in my pulpit, I have felt as if some great influence were at work in Markham. Is it the divine Spirit manifesting Himself in unusual power for some reason we cannot tell? What else could have prevailed upon Dean Randall to do such an astonishing thing as to invite you into the pulpit of Grace Cathedral?"

John nodded and urged him to go on.

"I have asked these questions many times lately," Harris said. "But when I came into my room here, I felt a presence that I could not deny. That is the reason my stay here was so long. I have never had a similar experience. If Christ is still alive, as we say we believe, He manifested Himself to me here in a way I cannot wholly explain. I saw no form, I heard no voice. But I was conscious of an appeal being made to me by some person who instantly became real to my thought as the Lord.

"It is hardly necessary for me to say," Harris continued, "that I have always been a very zealous Baptist. The last thing in the world that I once expected to do is what I have done today. I have always believed in and upheld our tradition that Communion should be limited to members of our church. But this morning, I was irresistibly influenced to invite you and your people to the Lord's Supper. I rebelled at first. But I could not leave the room. I knew the people were waiting for me to come out, but when I finally did yield, it seemed as if there was a sudden breaking into the room of a great light. I cannot deny the experience I had here an hour ago."

"It was the Holy Spirit," John said after a long silence. He had never felt so solemn, so profoundly moved. Was this the miracle at Markham that he had judged necessary for the union of the churches? If God was still at work in His world, and Christ still loved the church as he did two thousand years ago, why should His Spirit not intervene in a tangible way to encourage unity? Was the Holy Spirit unable to move a man or a city in this way? Of course not.

---

With this divine impulse gaining power, John went to the meeting the next evening that was to decide the future of the Congregational church in Markham. With seriousness and intensity, the people discussed for three hours every phase of the proposed union with some other church in town. The most prominent members had expressed themselves freely. Finally, one of the deacons, a man whose Christian character commanded the respect of every member of the church, rose and offered a formal motion.

"I move," he said with grave deliberation, "that our church take steps to unite with some other Christian church here in Markham, and that the details of such union be left to a committee, of which our pastor shall be the chairman."

The motion was seconded at once by one of the trustees. The congregation had been discussing such a motion all the evening. They were ready now to act upon it. John Procter, however, could not tell even yet, after all the evening's discussion, how the vote would go.

The vote was taken by ballot. Even while the ballots were being counted, there was none of the usual whispering and speculation common at such a time.

"The clerk is ready to announce the result of the ballot," said John, who rose and stood by the table where the counting had been going on.

"Total number of votes cast is one hundred thirty-two," said the clerk. "Of which seven are against the motion, and the balance, one hundred twenty-five, are in favor it."

The clerk's voice was generally a little indistinct, but every syllable he uttered now fell distinctly on the ears of the congregation. There was no applause, no shallow enthusiasm. The Congregational church had taken the most important step in all its history and it realized the solemnness of it.

John decided to say a few words. "Naturally, I wish the vote had been entirely unanimous. I am very glad, however, that it is practically so. I'm confident that time will prove the wisdom of our course. Let us join in prayer, asking the Spirit to lead us."

12.

# A Broken Heart

❦

FTER MUCH PRAYERFUL negotiation, the Congregational church and the Presbyterian church became one, commemorated and celebrated with a remarkable Communion service in which a dozen new members joined their ranks and professed faith in Christ.

To all of this, Dean Randall of the Episcopal church was a profoundly moved spectator, although he offered to preach several times at subsequent meetings. But events for the dean were moving on to a crisis. The action he had taken in asking John Procter to preach from his pulpit had not passed by unnoticed. One of his wardens had made formal complaint to the bishop. The bishop had, in turn, after another ineffectual appeal to the dean, reluctantly called on him to appear for trial before a church tribunal. This governing body was to convene on the coming Tuesday, six weeks after the union of the two churches.

The dean had grown visibly worn down and sadder since these events. On Saturday, one of the dean's parishioners, a man who loved and trusted him, came to see him about the trial.

"There is one point we have overlooked," he said, as he sat in the dean's study and noted with sorrow the dean's haggard appearance. "The cathedral has never been consecrated. You remember we are waiting to complete the guild hall and a part of the east nave. No church rule can possibly forbid you from inviting a clergyman of another denomination into an unconsecrated church building. In making your defense before the tribunal next Tuesday, you can take the ground that the cathedral has never been consecrated formally, and therefore, you had a perfect right to invite Brother Procter into Grace Cathedral."

The dean was obviously startled. He had forgotten the fact to which his parishioner called his attention.

"You're absolutely right," he replied. Then he was silent. It was a purely technical way of escaping from a difficulty. No church tribunal could hold him guilty on account of that technical fact. But had he no other or higher motive for what he had done?

The parishioner went out of the dean's study puzzled to know what he would do. He gave the impression that he did not intend to make use of the technical unconsecration of the cathedral when he appeared before the court.

Sunday, the people of Grace Cathedral all noted with an

almost-shocked surprise the manner of Dean Randall in the pulpit. He looked like a man who had received some great blow that had disturbed his whole nature. And still, not even his closest friends understood the mental agony the dean was enduring.

He sat in his study Tuesday morning. The trial had been fixed for ten o'clock. The clergymen and bishops summoned, had all arrived, and the occasion was one of deep interest to all Markham. The dean had asked his wife to leave him for a few moments by himself. He wanted to write out something. She had been very anxious about him that morning. He wanted a little while to be alone. He would be ready to go over to the cathedral in time, he said.

She went out reluctantly. As she looked back, the view she had of her husband was reassuring. He was sitting quietly at his desk, writing. She shut the door and went into the sitting room to wait for him. The minutes went by, and still the dean did not come out. It was five minutes after ten. Mrs. Randall became very nervous. She stole out into the hall and listened at the study door. No sound. The bell rang at that instant. The noise startled her.

A messenger at the door had been sent over from the cathedral to ask if the dean was ill. The report had been circulated that he might not be able to appear for trial. The tribunal was seated and ready for him. Mrs. Randall hesitated no longer. She opened the dean's study door softly, and took a step into the room.

The dean was still at his desk. What he had written lay neatly on the top of a prayer book. He had not taken his own life, but his face was lying on the picture of Christ in Gethsemane, which he had taken down from its usual position over his desk, and his spirit had departed to God who gave it, beyond the jurisdiction of all ecclesiastical courts of earthly power.

13.

# The Dean's Confession

❦

N THE THIRD DAY AFTER he was found dead in his study, the body of Dean Randall was buried in the cemetery out on the wooded hills by the river.

The funeral service in the cathedral was impressive. Many of the clergymen who had been summoned to the trial of the dean were present at his funeral. Bishop Park, with an unusually sad face, conducted the service, his voice breaking more than once. He loved Dean Randall, without altogether understanding him. Besides, as his eyes rested on the front seat near the chancel rail, he felt during all the service the presence of Francis Randall, who had come from Pyramid. His mother leaned upon him, her pale face turning often to him for comfort.

Out at the grave, she clasped her son's arm with both her hands, while the words were recited solemnly, "Earth to earth, ashes to ashes, dust to dust." Then, after the last friend had departed from their house that evening, they again read the letter the dean had written the day of his death. Francis held the sheets of paper in his hand and thoughtfully reread his father's confession. For that is what it really was.

> To my dear wife and my son, Francis,
>
> The statement that is found at the close of what I write here this morning was written several years ago. At the present time, this Tuesday morning, when I am awaiting the trial at the cathedral, I do not see anything in it to modify or withdraw. I wish my wife and son to read what I have here written and make public only such parts of it as they may find it wise to do. I have opened my whole heart to you. Some of my disclosure is too sacred for others. May the Lord of all grace and mercy keep and bless you. If I am summoned by the God of all life into His presence this day, I go prepared to meet His all-knowing and all-compassionate love. This is written in the faith that anticipates a joyful meeting.

It was at this point that the dean had evidently dropped his pen upon the paper. He had then risen, taken down the picture, placed the pages of his statement together, and then fallen on the desk, as his wife had found him when she entered the study.

The statement that followed what the dean had written that Tuesday morning was this:

I write the following in order that those who are nearest to me may understand; that may seem to many of them contrary to my nature, as they think they have known me for many years.

When the Rev. John Procter's church burned down and I invited him into the pulpit of Grace Cathedral, probably not one man among all my acquaintances in Markham understood my motive. It was not a sudden resolve on my part, but was in reality the result of the conviction of several years' experience and meditation, deepened and strengthened by the experience of my own son in his Western parish.

But since my invitation, which has led up to this trial that awaits me, I have had a strange and, to me, inexpressibly painful revolution of feeling and also of judgment.

Day by day the conviction has grown with me that I have made a mistake in this matter. I believe as firmly as ever in the great need of Christian union. I feel as if it was all wrong that our church should refuse to admit clergymen of other denominations into its pulpit to preach or administer the sacraments. But now my judgment begins to torture me by asserting that I have not chosen the best or wisest way to bring about change. I think that I should have either withdrawn from the Episcopal church altogether and united with some other where my convictions were compatible.

I have done neither of these things. My whole outward church life has made such a course as to make one of these impossible for me. I have therefore been tormented by the conviction that my attempt to bring about a spirit of Christian union has failed within my own church, while at the same time I have not acknowledged my mistake, nor withdrawn myself from the dilemma which has grown more perplexing to me with every day's approach to the trial.

As I write this, I do not see at all clearly what the future is for the Episcopal church, so far as any attempt toward real church union is concerned. If the time should come when the old canon law, forbidding other ministers to preach in our churches, should be withdrawn or modified, it would, without doubt, have a mighty influence upon the churches to bring them together.

I am without any hesitation whatever in saying this law is contrary to the spirit of Christ and ought not to be a part of the Episcopal church life. There is one other matter that concerns my family. For the last two years, I have looked death in the face daily. A lesion of the heart valves has made possible my sudden death at any time. My physician knows this. No one else. I have considered all sides of the possibility so far as my own wife and son are concerned. There would be no difference in my condition or in the chances for my recovery if I were to cease work. I am in no pain, and my end, when it comes, will probably be swift and without suffering. I think my wife and son will understand what I have tried to explain.

For a long time, Francis and his mother dwelled upon this remarkable revelation.

"Do you believe, Francis, that your father was really mistaken?" his mother asked. "I mean, did he make a real mistake when he invited John Procter into the cathedral?"

Mrs. Randall asked this question of her son with painful interest in his reply.

"Mother," said Francis thoughtfully, "I do not believe Father made any mistake. But it is the sad thing for us to know now that he believed he did. What he says about the best way to bring about a union between our church and others is vital. I have struggled over that question more than over any other. I do not yet see the light."

Before he went back to Pyramid, he went to see Jane Procter. He had not talked with her since his sad return. When he rang the bell, Jane herself opened the door. She had on her hat and cloak and seemed confused at the sight of Randall.

"Excuse me," said Francis gravely, "perhaps you were going out. Don't let me keep you if you were."

"No, no," stammered Jane, "I ... you ... I am very glad to see you. Won't you come in?"

Francis entered and followed Jane into the parlor. As he took a seat, Jane noticed that his hand, the one that had been burned, was quite disfigured. As she remembered, Francis had always taken pride in his physical appearance and was careful to look his best. She wondered how he felt now.

"Did you really mean that?" asked Randall, after an awkward pause.

"Mean what?" asked Jane, trembling to think he might have actually caught her looking at his damaged hand.

"Are you really glad to see me, Jane?" he asked. "Because you know what I have come for, don't you?"

"No, I don't," replied Jane, faintly.

Even as she said this, she thought, *If he proposes to me again, I do not know if I can refuse him.*

"You should know, Jane, that I feel just the same that I always did," he said. "You have no idea how I dread to go back to Pyramid alone. Do I need to tell you again that I love you with all my heart?"

Jane did not dare look up. Her heart beat fast. A great conflict was going on within her. She felt that if once she looked up into Francis's pale, handsome face, she would not be able to say no to him again.

He waited a moment for her to answer his question, and then slowly and deliberately picked up his chair and brought it over close to her and sat down. He did not move to touch her, and something told Jane that he would never attempt even a caress until she had yielded her heart to him. But when he spoke again, she trembled at the thought of the man's great love for her.

"Jane, I cannot and I will not go back to Pyramid until I know whether you love me," he said. "You must tell me. Do you love me, Jane, or not?"

"I have told you I cannot marry a minister." Jane's lips trembled and her voice was low. "I am not suited for such a life."

"That is not my question," said Francis firmly, and still Jane did not dare to look up at him.

But something in his tone roused a feeling of resistance in Jane's nature.

"Ministers live such dull, self-sacrificing lives," she responded. "I am tired of the sacrifices demanded of a poor minister's daughter. I could never make you happy."

A great change came into Francis's face. He clenched his hands on the chair, as if to keep himself from falling. The scar on his right hand stood out like a terrible birthmark. His large, soft eyes grew hard and the whole man stiffened as if in sudden resistance to a blow.

He rose from his seat and stood directly in front of Jane. She seemed compelled to look up at him.

"So you will not marry me because I am a poor minister? Is that it?" he asked. "It is not because I am in the church, but because I am not rich?"

Jane would not answer, but her tongue seemed powerless. The unexpected disclosure of her secret reason, which she had not even dared to acknowledge to herself except at rare moments, filled her heart with fear and shame.

He waited a moment, and then said, "You have given me your answer."

Before she could realize what he was doing, he had turned and walked swiftly out of the parlor into the hall. He opened the door and went out. Then Jane ran into the hall.

As she ran, she cried out with a sob, "No, no, Francis! I do love you!" She even had her hand on the door and was about to open it, but a feeling of shame seized her and she went back into the parlor and, throwing herself down on the couch, cried as she had not cried since she was a little girl.

14.

# A United Campaign

❦

IT IS POSSIBLE THAT IF FRANCIS had heard her he might have come back. But the man's heart was breaking within him, and he left for Pyramid with a great sadness of soul.

As he took up the burdens of his rough-and-tumble parish, he groaned in spirit and asked himself if it was worthwhile to make the struggle. Nothing but his Christian faith now kept him true to the routine of duties that must be obeyed, whether his human heart was satisfied or not. It was one comfort to him that his mother went with him to keep house for him temporarily.

As for Jane, she confronted for the first time her real motive for refusing to marry Francis. The hideous fact that she was forced to face was doubly bad to her, because she had thought to deceive herself for a long time by keeping it in the background. But had she given Francis her final answer? She loved him more than ever. Only that gaunt, troublesome thing—the poverty and meagerness of a poor minister's house—seemed to thrust in between her heart's longing and her lover's persistence. In the days that followed, she went to her school with the treadmill pace of one who has seen heaven draw very near, and then vanish, with no hope or desire for the future.

---

Francis, far from the glow of any religious enthusiasm, such as now began to light up the church in Markham as a result of the extraordinary union, fought his way through his parish duties like a man stricken with disease of all his faculties. William was quick to notice the change in his friend. They were friends now, for William knew what he owed the young clergyman. He noted with regret the change in the once-eager step and buoyant bearing, and wondered at its cause.

One evening, about two months after Francis's return to Pyramid, he came into William's room, where he was still convalescing and beginning to think of getting to work again. Randall had a letter in his hand.

"Read that," he said.

William read and exclaimed in wonder, "Why, they want you to come to Grace Cathedral! Your father's old church in Markham!"

"Yes, the bishop wants me to take a place under the new dean. The congregation has asked for me."

"And you'll go, right?" asked William, feeling at the

same time a pang of loneliness at the thought of Randall leaving Pyramid.

"I don't know," replied Randall slowly, as he turned a log of wood over in the open fireplace they were sitting in front of. "I don't think I shall. I don't care to go to Markham." And he was very quiet after that. The fire from the logs threw strange shadows upon Francis's face, but the real shadow was on his heart, and he wondered if it ever would be chased away by the light of love again.

15.

# Francis's Return to Markham

❦

WO MONTHS LATER, JOHN came into the parsonage one evening just before tea time and surprised his wife and daughter by saying, "I just met Dean Murray. He says Francis Randall has written accepting the position in the cathedral and expects to leave Pyramid when his year there is up, around Christmas."

Jane was standing by the table when her father spoke. During those dreary weeks that followed Francis's departure from Markham, she had gone about her school duties stubbornly but without any heart in them. The announcement of Francis's proposed return to Markham affected her, at first in a way she was not prepared for. She could feel her heart beating fast, and her mind was confused as to what her lover's return might mean to her. She wanted to ask her father a question, but dared not trust her voice to do so. Her mother spoke at that moment, as Jane turned from the table and slowly walked into the kitchen.

"What place will he hold under Dean Murray?" Kate asked.

"He will undertake the parish work, I believe," replied John. Then he added in a low voice, although Jane had shut the kitchen door when she went out, "I am sorry Francis is coming here. I am sure it means trouble for Jane. She has not been the same girl since the dean's death. I mean, since young Randall was last here. Has she confided in you?"

"No," replied Kate, with a sigh. "There is something Jane will not tell me. I know she loves Francis, and something has happened to make her sad. But she has not told me what it is."

At that moment, Jane was saying to herself out in the kitchen as she tried to hold back the tears, *I'm sorry he is coming. How can I bear to meet him, after what has happened?*

---

Several motives had urged Francis to return to Markham. The new dean was a man who had known and sympathized with Dean Randall. The death of the dean had caused a change of sentiment throughout the parish. Francis knew enough about him to be sure that, so far as working out the problem of church union was concerned, Dean Murray would not stand in the way of any reasonable attempts.

But the primary motive that influenced Francis was a personal desire to face the worst and work through it. If he returned to Markham and met Jane, he might grow, in time, to realize that the loss of her was not so great as now he felt it to be. Many times he had thought that, if Jane really refused to be his wife because he was poor, her character was not strong enough to help him in his lifework. If she placed so much importance on money, then perhaps she was not the person of integrity he had once believed her to be.

He finally resolved to go back to Markham and see if the chance of constantly seeing Jane would convince him, after all, that they were not right for each other. In any case he was so restless and unhappy in his work at Pyramid, that he felt that his usefulness there was almost gone.

When he had finally made up his mind, he told William, as they sat again in front of the fire, "I'm going back to Markham, after all."

William looked at him wistfully and at last he said, "Of course I don't blame you to want a better place than this. Pyramid is not exactly Markham and Grace Cathedral."

"It isn't just that," replied Francis slowly. "The fact is, I have lost my interest in this work out here. I want to say to you, Will, that I, well … never mind. I can't tell you, but I feel the need of a change, and that's the reason I'm going to Markham."

William did not ask any questions. A recent letter from his mother had revealed a part of Jane's story, and William knew something of the cause for Francis's decision. He did not dare to intrude or press his friend to reveal the whole truth. And, in fact, Francis could not confide the truth to anyone, least of all to Jane's brother.

When the time came for Francis's departure, Pyramid

realized what it was about to lose. William Procter felt it deeper than others.

"You'll have to take up my fight against the gambling dens, Will," said Francis, as he walked over to the train station the day he left. He spoke with a sad smile, but he had no idea that his words carried any weight with them or were really taken in earnest by his friend.

But when Francis had gone, and William turned back to his little room and remembered that he was to resume his mill duties, he was unable to shake off the impression that, somehow, in some way, he was responsible for a part of Pyramid's moral life.

With the conviction that he would be carried, in spite of himself, into the fight that Francis had begun, he walked into the mill the next day. It was not without a curious blending of emotions that he stopped at the entrance of the mixing room and looked again upon the place where he had so nearly met his death. That day, two voices called to him: the voice of duty to the camp that had lost its champion of truth and right, and the voice of his love for a woman in Andover who had lost her love for him.

---

The week before Christmas, John said one evening, as he came in from his work, "I met Francis Randall today. He has just returned."

"How is he?" Kate asked the question, while Jane made a miserable effort to appear unconcerned, as she went on with some piece of sewing. But her fingers trembled and her face flushed.

"Why, I think he looks about the same," replied John. "I only saw him for a moment."

That was about all that was said, but the next morning when Jane started toward school, she faced the possibility of meeting Francis on the street. She usually walked past the cathedral on her way to school. It was the shortest way. But this morning she went several blocks out of the way and felt relieved when she did not see him. It was several days before she met Francis, and then it happened so suddenly that she had no time to determine what she should do.

It was one afternoon, as she stepped out of the schoolroom after the day's work was done. She was tired and had a headache. But that was nothing compared to the heartache that pained her now every day. The children were swarming all about her, and she was walking slowly. Suddenly, Francis turned the corner and passed her.

As he went by, he lifted his hat. Jane had wondered, several times, whether he would ignore her entirely. But he was too much of a gentleman to do that, and besides, had he not once loved her with all his heart? Jane knew that he had looked at her as he went by. Still, he had walked straight on, and without the slightest hesitation.

So that was the way they were to meet hereafter? Simply as bowing acquaintances? Jane had a momentary feeling of relief, that she knew now what to expect. At the same time she cried harder that night than at any time since her last talk with him.

As for Francis, he neither avoided nor sought any

opportunity for seeing Jane that winter. As a matter of fact, they did meet at a few social gatherings, but at none of them did they ever exchange a word. Francis went out very little. His ministry duties occupied nearly every evening, and it was only when his church responsibility compelled him that he appeared in public. It soon began to be rumored in Markham that the popular assistant to the dean was writing a book, but what it was, whether history or religion or a love story, no one seemed to know.

It is quite certain that never in all its history had Markham experienced such a change in its church life from the time Francis entered the Grace Cathedral parish. Whatever may have been the depth of his personal disappointment, the hunger and restlessness of his heart, there was no question as to his willingness to help make the union of the churches in Markham a reality.

John Procter and Hugh Cameron soon discovered that an added force had entered Markham with the coming of Francis. He was heartily in sympathy with the work they had undertaken to unite the churches, confront the saloons of the town, and establish a Christian newspaper.

*16.*

# An Interview with Father Morris

❦

RANCIS AGREED TO SURVEY the other pastors to see where they all stood on matters of common interest. When he had completed his round of the churches, he reported to John Procter and Hugh Cameron.

"The fact is," he said after they had discussed the matter, "there is practical unanimity among the churches as to the need of taking action together."

"How about Father Morris?" asked Hugh Cameron.

"What? The Catholic priest?" asked Francis, starting and looking earnestly at the Presbyterian minister.

"I hadn't thought of him," said John. They were all three silent a moment. The Catholic priest had almost always remained separate from all other churches in

Markham, and he kept his congregation that way too.

"Francis, do you know Father Morris?" Hugh asked.

"My father knew him quite well," he replied. "He once did Morris a great favor. Mother mentioned it the other day. I'll go and see him, if you say so, and find out if he will act with us."

"It will not do any harm and may do much good," said John, thoughtfully. "He has a large influence over some of the factory people."

"I'll go and see him," said Francis as he went away.

He did not find time to make the call until Saturday of that week, and he approached the priest's house and anticipated the interview with him in a spirit of greater curiosity and excitement than he had felt for a long time.

Francis waited some time before the priest appeared. Father Morris was clean-shaven and wore the dress of the Catholic church. Around his neck hung a slender gold chain with a small white cross fastened to it. His face was pale, but when he smiled, it became animated and even dignified. He was a small man, and next to Francis he seemed even smaller.

He came slowly into the parlor and Francis waited for him to speak.

"Pardon me, I did not understand from the servant the name?" the priest said with a stiffness that may have been habitual or simply suited to his feelings at the time.

"Randall, Rev. Francis Randall. I am Dean Murray's assistant at Grace Cathedral. You knew my father, Dean Randall, though I don't believe you and I have ever met before."

"Oh!" the priest said with a swift and almost suspicious look at Francis. "Please sit down. Yes, I knew your father quite well."

"I have come on a somewhat singular errand, Father Morris," he began. "But I feel sure you will listen to it kindly when I tell you that your church will benefit by what I want to propose to you."

Again that look of suspicion crossed the priest's face, and he looked at Francis doubtfully. "Is it in reference to the money your father loaned me several years ago?"

It was Francis's turn to look surprised. He knew his father had helped the priest at a time of difficulty. There were no papers recording the transaction, except a memorandum of the dean's that Francis and his mother had found several days after the dean's death. Francis did not know the circumstances under which the priest obtained the money, nor how far the acquaintance between his father and the priest had passed. He only knew the amount of the loan was large and had never been paid back.

"No, I did not come to see you about that," he said, looking directly at the priest. "My father had no record, other than a statement of the fact."

Father Morris looked a little uneasily at Francis. Then his face softened, and he seemed to show, for the first time, his real nature underneath the liturgical dress and the chain and cross.

"Mr. Randall," he said with sincerity, "years ago your father loaned me a sum of money that saved my old mother and two sisters in Limerick from starving. It was during the famine of 1876. That money has been saved during all these years, and I now have nearly the entire sum and will pay it back to you within a year."

Francis looked at the man in astonishment. There was more here than appeared on the surface. But the priest had told all that he was ready to tell.

"Really, I did not come in regard to any financial matters," Francis said. He went on rapidly to tell of the action already taken by the other ministers and churches, and asked whether the priest might be counted on to join them, beginning with their efforts to move Markham to observe Sunday as the Sabbath more strictly.

It was a significant pause that followed. Francis was wondering if Father Morris hesitated because he did not want to take directions for church work from a man outside the Catholic faith.

"Yes, I am willing to do that," the answer came at last. "Of course, you understand, Mr. Randall, we do not hold to the strict interpretation of Sunday that prevails in many Protestant Communions?"

"I have to confess my ignorance largely of your views," replied Francis with a smile.

"It makes no difference," the older man said. "I will undertake to make my people see the needs of which you speak. There is no question that many of them are foolishly spending their time and money in Sunday amusements."

Francis felt that his point had been gained, but he ventured one more step.

"Father Morris, when the other churches begin soon, as they are planning to do, a campaign against the saloons in Markham, will you and your church join us in that fight?"

The change that swept over the priest's face was startling. His lower jaw stiffened, the hands clenched tight on the arms of the chair, and the emphasis of his reply left nothing to be desired on Francis's part.

"So help me God, Randall, I will join you or any other man in common cause against the drink traffic. Have I not been for years pleading with my people to let the stuff alone? Yet not even the power of the Catholic church has availed here in this town, to stay this sin. Is your Protestant church guiltless of sin in the matter of licensing and supporting the saloons?"

"Certainly not—to our shame," replied Francis. He was simply astonished at the priest's answer.

He went out on the street in a conflict of emotions. The interview had surprised him. There was more in Father Morris than he had supposed. Connected with the loan of the money was some tragic occurrence deeper even than the one mentioned by the priest. The effort he had been making all these years to pay the money back proved him to be honest. And the priest's insistence that he would join efforts with the other churches stirred Francis, John, and Hugh to greater hopefulness. They began to see something now of the dawn of new days for Markham.

*17.*

# New Directions

ISS REBECCA PHILLIPS SAT IN the room next to her father's study one winter evening, trying to read a novel. The professor was in his study, still laboring over his notes for the volume on the minor prophets.

It was a wild winter night in Andover. The snow lay very deep on the hill, and the wind was tossing the branches of the great elms out in front of the seminary buildings. The evening mail was late. But at last the boy who carried it to the professors' houses rang the bell, and Rebecca answered it.

She came back into the sitting room with a newspaper sent from Markham. The name and address were in Jane Procter's handwriting. Rebecca sat down in front of the open fireplace and slowly tore off the wrapper and unfolded the paper. It was the *Pyramid Miner* and dated only a few days back. She turned at once to the article in the paper that was marked and read the following:

> William Procter, who has been assistant superintendent of the Golconda, Sewell's Mill, has given up his position there, and taken to preaching.

Rebecca stared at the sentence hard, and read it again. She was sorely agitated by the fact that William was actually preaching. Under what conditions and difficulties, she could only vaguely guess. But the old quarrel that had resulted in the breaking of her engagement seemed to her, under this new movement, to be insufficient. She had judged William hastily when he decided to give up the ministry. She had judged him to be lacking in strength of decision. But she had never ceased to love him. Would this action on William's part make possible their union at some time?

She did not take the paper in to show her father. But she sat by the fire a long time with her hands folded on her lap. The professor's pen scratched away on the manuscript. The wind roared over the hill. And Rebecca looked into the fire and wondered if the future would bring to her again the joy that once she knew.

---

That same winter brought to Francis also an experience that shaped his work and decided, in a large measure, his future. He had never been so busy. The growing union of the churches in Markham had given him an opportunity to use his powers in a great variety of ways. He had plunged into his work of church union with a tremendous energy that helped him, so he thought, to forget Jane. In reality, he never forgot her. He saw her seldom. But deep down in his heart the old fire burned.

There were, however, times when he grew absorbed in his writing. It was one more attempt on his part to provide his head and heart with a diversion. How far he had succeeded with the book, he could not tell. He had never written a long story, and felt unable to pronounce objective judgment on his own work.

He had grown to love his characters, and with a regret that was excusable, he wrote the last sentence and after a fashion said good-bye to the hero and heroine whom he had happily married after a long and difficult series of situations. He was sitting in his little room and beginning to wonder if any publisher would accept the book, and if so, whether the public would find it worth reading.

Just then, his mother knocked at the door. "My dear," she said, as Francis rose and opened the door and insisted on her coming in and taking the one easy chair in the room. "Have you heard the news from Mr. Procter?"

"No, Mother," Francis answered, and a sudden fear clutched at his heart, and he turned cold and trembling.

"Your father's old friend Dr. Gilbert just stopped to say that Jane is very ill with typhoid. A sudden and serious case. Francis, my heart aches for you! Can even your mother comfort you?"

"No," replied Francis. He looked with dull eyes at his book, which he had just finished, and then at his mother.

And his heart reproached him. Of what value was his book to him now? Or anything else?

"I did not mean that, Mother," he said after a pause. Then he sat down suddenly and put his head between his hands. A moment later, he stood and went out into the hall. He looked at the clock, which read ten o'clock. Then he peered out the window to see a snowstorm beginning.

Putting on his coat and hat, he said, "I'm going over to John Procter's to inquire about Jane." With that, he went out into the storm.

18.

# A Message for Jane

HEN FRANCIS SHUT THE door of his house and started through that gathering snowstorm toward the Procters' home, the tumult in his heart and mind was far greater than the physical tempest that howled around him.

Fight against the feeling as he might, he knew that he still loved Jane. The news of her sudden and serious illness gripped his heart with a force that emphasized the slumbering passion of his life, and told him, that right or wrong, he had not been able to shut her out as unworthy.

Had he misjudged her? He had given her no chance to reply to him or defend herself from the charge that he had made—the charge that it was because he was poor that she would not marry him. How did he know, after all, that she had not spoken that one sentence thoughtlessly and impulsively? And yet he had condemned her swiftly, at once, and without leaving her any possible opportunity to defend herself.

When at last he reached the Procters' house, he saw that the light was burning in John's study. Francis went to the side door and knocked. John opened the door, and at the sight of Francis, he uttered an exclamation of surprise.

"I heard that Jane was very ill," he said. "I came to check on her."

"Come in," said John, who understood at once the situation.

Francis entered the study and sat down, and as he had done when his mother announced the news, he put his head between his hands for a moment. He then looked up and spoke steadily, looking John full in the face.

"I hardly need to tell you, Mr. Procter, that I have loved Jane for several years. You may know also that there has been a misunderstanding between us. I find that it has not changed my feelings. I've heard she was dangerously ill."

"Yes, she is dangerously ill," repeated John gravely. "We pray for the best, but must prepare for the worst."

"I understand," Francis said in a voice filled with emotion. "I don't know that I can do anything, but I had to come. What does the doctor say?"

"The doctor says there is some hope." But John spoke without hope himself, and Francis was quick to note this.

There was silence between the two men.

Kate suddenly came into the study. She greeted Francis without much surprise. Indeed, the mother knew everything, at least, all except Jane's miserable secret about that last encounter with the young man. Already in her delirium, Jane had said more than once, "I do love you, Francis!"

"Jane has been working extremely hard in school lately," said Kate, in answer to some question which Francis involuntarily asked. "When the breakdown came at last, it was very sudden."

John had slipped out of the room. Francis rose, and Mrs. Procter held out both her hands to him. He took them and told her what he had told John and more. Only, he could not tell quite all. That seemed like Jane's secret.

Kate tried to comfort him. But she was confused. The probability of Jane's death increased, rather than lessened, her doubt as to what she ought to reveal of Jane's remarks in her unconscious condition.

"Will you tell Jane one thing, Mrs. Procter?" asked Francis, after a pause. He hesitated but went on firmly. "If she recovers consciousness, will you tell her that I still love her, that I have not been able to put her out of my heart?"

With tears running down her face, Kate replied, "Yes, I will tell her."

Francis prepared to go out into the storm.

"We will let you know the moment there is a change," Kate said.

---

Outside in the blowing snow, Francis stopped at the corner and looked back at the lighted upper window where he knew Jane was lying. The woman he loved was there dying. He looked a long time, oblivious to the storm. Then he slowly went home, and the whole force of the white storm suddenly seemed to weigh him down.

In the days that followed, Francis did many things, mechanically, from force of habit, as he had trained himself to do them. Among other things, he sent his book to a well-known publishing firm in New York and then forgot all about it. His interest in the book had died out of him from that night when he first learned of Jane's illness.

Before long, a time of crisis arose. One night, when a storm broke again over Markham, and drifted great banks of snow through the streets, the weary watchers by Jane's bedside noted a change that marks the soul's approach to the mysterious otherworld. The forces of the body and spirit had struggled long for mastery. The wan faces of nurse and mother, the stern sadness of the father and doctor, witnessed the culmination of the struggle. And at last as dawn broke through the storm, Jane's body and spirit finally triumphed over the illness. Those who loved her knew that she would live. When the doctor said that the crisis was passed, and life had conquered, her parents broke down and wept. John went into his study, and Kate soon followed him there. After a moment of rejoicing together and prayers of thanksgiving, they sent word to Francis.

His mother brought him the news, and he received it in silence. His heart went out in a great wave of praise to God.

After a moment, he said, "Mother, our heavenly Father has spared her for some good reason."

"I pray He has spared her that you may have joy again," she responded.

During the next few hours, he wondered if Kate would tell Jane what he had asked her to. The first time he called at the house, Kate told him that she had not said anything to Jane yet.

"Do you want me to say anything now?" Kate asked, as Francis looked at her with a troubled expression.

"No. I think it would be better, on the whole, not to," replied Francis.

Then he went back to his work, feeling that Jane's illness had not really changed the relationship that existed before. It had emphasized his love for her, but could he assume any change had happened to Jane?

In this uncertainty, he simply did what a man of his simple-hearted nature would do—he took up his work again, and waited. If Jane ever changed, ought she not, in some way, to let him know it? Could he, in any case, again presume upon the possibility that she might love him? It might place her in a critical position, but somehow he felt that he must wait for her to let him know what the future was to be.

During this time, while Jane was slowly recovering, word came one day to Francis that his book had been accepted by the publishers. It was a surprise to him. He had anticipated refusal. He at once wrote, accepting the terms specified by the publisher. Then, in the time while the book was being prepared for the public, he again forgot it largely, or at least he did not have any great hopes of its popular success.

One reason for this feeling, or lack of feeling, rare in a young author over his first book, was due to the events which made Markham famous that winter. For the reform begun by the churches had swept Markham like a fire. Even the sneering comments of the daily paper had not been able to stop the tide that rose and overwhelmed all opposition.

19.

# A Paper in Markham

❦

As the winter was drawing to its close, the Christian community in Markham began to realize that it was entering upon a new and unusual era. The churches had, to their surprise, found that they had a common meeting ground in the sacredness of the Sabbath.

It was no unusual thing for John Procter, Charles Harris, Capt. Andrews of the Salvation Army, Francis Randall, and Rev. Lawrence Brown, the Methodist minister, to speak from the same platform at a meeting in which the question was discussed from all sides.

Even as momentum gained in the unity among churches, John conceived an idea to further reinforce high moral standards and Christian character in the town. A daily newspaper owned and controlled by the churches was the idea that John constantly held up to the people. He finally succeeded in gaining over to his view nearly every pastor in Markham. The idea was a new one, but its very originality appealed to the churchpeople.

"We need such a paper," John would say, "before we can make any successful fight against the saloons in Markham." He repeatedly pointed out the fact that the only daily that Markham had was committed wholly to the promotion of the alcohol industry and the establishments that sold it. He also emphasized the need of a paper in the homes of Markham that would represent and support the principles taught in the churches.

"If the daily paper is tearing down six days in a week," John argued, "a great part of what the preachers are trying to build up one day, how much headway can we make against the saloons or any form of evil? We must have some daily voice of Christian conviction sounding in the ears of our people to supplement the words we speak to them from the pulpit."

In time, many of the businessmen of Markham began to respond. An effort was begun to raise funds to organize a daily paper that would be owned and controlled by Christian people. It was to be called *The Markham Union.*

---

Winter was over, and spring had really come at last. Francis was feeling better than he had once thought possible, after the most severe winter's work he had ever known. Somehow, he seemed to think all would come right between Jane and himself after all. He had not seen her often, had not spoken to her, but the few times he had caught glimpses of her she seemed to be recovering her health and beauty. Once at a social gathering his eyes had met hers, and she had blushed and turned pale again. Was it possible she had discovered the facts about his coming to the house while she was ill? Surely, Kate could not keep all that secret from her.

One day, Francis received in the mail a letter from his New York publisher, which read:

> Dear Mr. Randall,
>
> The sales of your book have just surpassed the five thousand mark, and orders are coming in rapidly. The outlook is very promising for a large and popular sale. We have ordered another five thousand at once from the printer. Telegraph us if you have any suggestions to make as to changes in preface or cover design. We congratulate you on your success.

Francis would have been less than human if he had not been thrilled at the contents of this letter. The possibility of what he had written going beyond a first small edition had never occurred to him. He had no exalted ideas of his abilities as a writer. But he was pleased. He read the letter over again and again.

An hour later, as he headed off for an appointment, he saw Jane coming up the street. This time she was not alone. A young man was walking by her, and as the two passed Francis, Jane's face burned red. The young man returned Francis's greeting, courteously, and passed on, still talking earnestly to Jane.

For the first time in his life, the Episcopal clergyman felt blaze up in him a passion of almost hatred. He knew Mark Wilson, the young lawyer who had grown up in Markham and moved to Columbus, Ohio, to take a position with a prestigious law firm. Francis had heard only good things about him, but at that moment he felt only disdain at the thought of this young man and Jane together.

"Hello, Jane," Francis said as casually as he could. "And hello, Mark. Fancy running into you. I'm just off to see your mother."

They exchanged brief pleasantries and parted just as quickly.

*She has given me her answer, though*, Francis kept saying to himself, as he doggedly went on toward Mrs. Wilson's. *The other man has money enough—or his family does, at least. If she wants to marry for money, she has an opportunity.*

Mrs. Wilson was genuinely glad to see him. She had been a firm friend of his father and one of his heartiest supporters in all the financial part of the church work. Francis presented the matter of the proposed Christian newspaper and was going into detail when Mrs. Wilson stopped him.

"You needn't say any more," she said. "I believe in all that. Put me down for a thousand dollars, and when you want more, call again."

Francis thanked her, and after some light conversation, he rose to go.

"Wait a minute, Mr. Randall, won't you?" asked Mrs. Wilson, sounding a little embarrassed. "I want to ask your advice about Mark."

"Yes?" said Francis, sitting down again, and feeling vaguely that something like a crisis had come to him.

"The fact is that Mark is desperately in love with Jane Procter," she explained. "He has been in love many times, but this time he is completely swept away. I don't know that I blame him. She is the prettiest and most sensible girl in Markham. I'll do anything I can to help Mark. He hasn't seen her for very long, only about two weeks now. He thinks her father and mother don't think too highly of him. Could you use your influence in any way with them? I want so much for him to be happy. I would do anything in the world for him. You know he will inherit all I have when I'm gone. He has all he wants now, for that matter."

Mrs. Wilson had talked on in her usual rapid fashion, wholly absorbed in the subject and not noticing Francis's face. She turned toward him, smiling. As for Francis, his expression had turned from agreeable to distraught in a matter of seconds. Mrs. Wilson was astonished at what she saw in his face. And she was still more astonished at his reply when he finally spoke.

20.

# What the King Said

RS. WILSON," SAID FRANCIS, looking straight at her and speaking slowly, "I cannot do what you ask, for the reason that I love Jane Procter myself."

Mrs. Wilson stared at him in astonishment. It was some time before she could say a word. "Of course, I knew nothing of all this, Mr. Randall," she said at last. "You know I have been away from Markham a great deal, and no one ever hinted such a thing to me."

It was true that Francis's romance had escaped the notice of the gossips in almost a miraculous manner. His time away in Pyramid, his apparent indifference to Jane when he returned to Markham, and the two families' silence had resulted in the absence of all talk about the matter.

"At the same time," said Francis, trying hard to conceal the emotion welling up within him, "I ought to tell you that I have no reason to hope Miss Procter will ever—"

He stopped suddenly, and Mrs. Wilson finished the sentence silently. She was beginning to understand the gravity and complexity of the situation.

For several seconds, neither of them spoke. Then Mrs. Wilson said, "Well, there isn't much either of us can do to prevent my son from trying to win Jane Procter. Mark is already in love with her. He has told me that he intends to ask her to be his wife. I am sure he will do this before he returns to Columbus next week. Even the knowledge of your love for her would make no difference with him. In fact, it would probably only hasten his action."

Francis looked up. "It is for her to choose. As you say, your son is rich. He is also ambitious and successful in his profession. What more could a woman ask?"

He spoke proudly, but there was a bitterness in his tone that Mrs. Wilson picked up on. She was a shrewd woman of the world, and it did not take much insight for her to discover a large part of Francis's secret.

"Naturally, I'll ask you to disregard what I said earlier about mentioning something to Mr. and Mrs. Procter," she said. "I did not realize …" Her voice trailed off.

"Of course," said Francis with quiet dignity. "And you respect my secret?"

"As if my life depended on it," replied Mrs. Wilson. To Francis, she sounded more than a little sad and perplexed.

Once out on the street, he had time to think over the whole matter. He walked around until it was dark. The picture of Jane and Mark Wilson together stood out vividly before him. He was torn with passion and tormented at the thought of Jane's probable reply to the rich young lawyer.

In spite of the fact that he had repeatedly said that Jane's answer in his own case was final and that they could never again be anything to each other, he agonized at the thought of another man winning her.

*If she accepts Mark's proposal,* he thought finally, *I shall know it is because she values wealth more than love. If she rejects him, I shall know that possibly there is hope for us yet.*

He walked quietly into his study without letting his mother know he was home. As he took off his overcoat, he remembered the letter he had received that afternoon, announcing the success of his first book. He took the letter out and threw it down on his desk. It meant less than nothing to him at that moment. And in the excitement and unrest of his feelings, he sat down, and laying his head on the desk with his face touching the letter that predicted his coming fame as an author, he groaned in spirit over his love for Jane.

---

The next few days were days of great uncertainty for Francis. More than once he met Jane and Mark Wilson on the street. Each time, Jane gave no indication of her feelings for the young lawyer. As for Mark, he did not attempt to disguise or hide his love for her. All the gossips in Markham were talking about the two, and it was the general opinion that Jane would marry him. Indeed, it was asserted that they were already engaged, which accounted for the fact that they were seen so often in each other's company.

Saturday of that week, as Francis was going home from a conference with Hugh Cameron, he passed by Mrs. Wilson's house. She saw him going by and tapped on the window and beckoned him to come in.

"Mark has gone back to Columbus," she began with a sad smile. "He received his answer. Jane Procter refused him."

Francis immediately felt a profound sense of relief.

"Of course," continued Mrs. Wilson, "I do not expect you to offer me any sympathy under the circumstances. It is a hard blow for Mark. It will take him a long time to get over it. I can't blame you for the way you must feel now."

"It is difficult for me to express myself, Mrs. Wilson. I am still—"

In fact, Francis was in the dark largely as to Jane's motives in refusing to accept Mark's proposal. Only this much was clear. She had positively refused an offer of marriage from a rich man. So, after all, money alone could not satisfy her.

Saying this over to himself, Francis went home, and with the beginning of the old hope again he faced his future. Should he speak to Jane again?

The following week he hesitated several times in the midst of his work and did not know what he ought to do. Once, he had met Jane on the street, and the blush on her face was readily apparent. After he had passed her a few steps, he did what he had never done before. He turned around and looked at her. As he did so, Jane also looked back at him. Then she hurried on faster than ever, and he went on slowly to his study, in more turmoil than he had been before.

The next morning, he received another letter from his publisher in New York, urging him to come and confer about future writing projects. He felt the need of a little change after the hard winter's work and also hoped that during the time he was away he might come to some right conclusion as to his attitude toward Jane, and that night he took the express for New York.

The next day Kate called at the Randall household regarding some church business and while there learned of Francis's departure.

"I understand his book has been very successful," Kate said. "Is that true?"

"Yes, it has been a wonderful success, according to the publishers," replied Mrs. Randall proudly. "And by the way, Francis left a copy here for John. Will you give it to him?"

Later, she could not help noticing Jane's look when her father took the book and read the title: *What the King Said*.

"It's an odd title," John remarked as he turned the pages. Like everyone else who saw it, he was curious to know what the book was about.

"It has had wonderful sales already," said Kate, and again she noted Jane's strange expression.

"Yes," continued John as he turned back to the beginning of the book and began to read, "I suppose Francis will make more than most authors make, on account of the strong sales."

"Do you suppose he could become rich from the book?" Kate asked, looking furtively at Jane.

"It's possible, I suppose," replied John.

Jane rose and went quickly out of the room.

---

The next day when John came in from his parish work, he could not find the book that he had left on his study table. He asked his wife where it was, and she said she thought Jane had taken it. In fact, at that moment, Jane, in her room, where she had gone immediately after school, was absorbed in the story. More than once her eyes filled with tears. Once she laid the book down and put her face in her hands with the gesture familiar to her. Then she opened the book and went on eagerly. This man, once her lover, was farther from her now than ever. He had written a successful book. He was growing not only famous, but probably rich. Even if in some way she were to let him know that she cared more for his love than for all the money in the world, how could he be sure that she was not now attracted by his probable fame and wealth?

So she sat reading on, her heart divided between admiration for the story, and love for its author, and uncertainty concerning the future. And of all the interested readers who that year acknowledged the fascination of the new book *What the King Said* it is safe to say none devoured its pages with the emotion that was felt by Jane Procter.

21.

# The Professor Visits Pyramid

❦

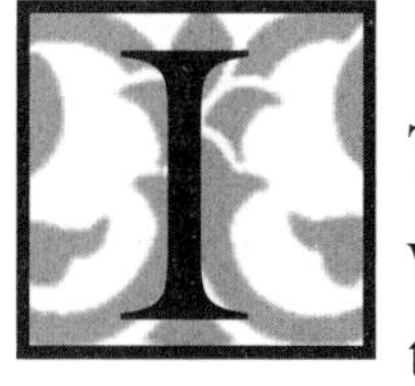

T WAS DURING THIS PERIOD while Francis was still absent in New York that William, out in Pyramid, fought his great fight and came to know the stress and bitterness of standing almost alone in a good cause. He was living on the earnings of his pay as superintendent of the mill, but that would soon be gone, and then he must find some means of keeping out of debt.

William's meetings were popular, and Mr. Clark, the minister who had befriended Francis, came to his assistance nobly. But before the public meetings had been running three days, Mr. Clark was stricken down with a serious illness, and after that, William carried on the fight almost alone.

Almost the entire sentiment of the camp was against him. The only paper printed in Pyramid, while not openly opposed to the meetings, concealed its indifference to the result under a sneer that gave the impression of support for the gambling element. Nevertheless, with a dogged persistence that characterized his father, William went on with his meetings. He at least had an audience. As long as people came, he was determined to preach to them.

For the first time since he had left the seminary, he felt at peace with himself. Whenever he thought of Rebecca Phillips, he could not crowd down a feeling of hope. He had not heard a word from her during all his illness. The telegram that had come so unexpectedly had been the only communication. Would he ever see her or hear from her again? He asked the question many times, even during the excitement of his meetings, and while he found no answer, somehow he lived in hope that Rebecca would some time be his again.

At this time in William's experience, Professor Elias Phillips came into the sitting room of his house in Andover with a letter, a part of which he read to Rebecca.

"It seems," he went on commenting on the letter, "that the mines at Capstone are beginning to produce unexpected ore. The shares I bought there years ago are now above par. The superintendent writes me to come if I can and investigate matters a little. Then there are the mines in Pyramid that have been in the courts so long. He says it would be good if I could come and see to my interests in person. I have been thinking—" The professor removed his spectacles and looked thoughtfully at Rebecca. "I have been thinking it would be best to make the trip, and I have been wondering if you would care to go with me."

Rebecca looked up at her father and her face burned. What would William think if she should suddenly appear in Pyramid? But, on the other hand, why should she not go if she wanted to?

"We could go as soon as next week—during the spring vacation," the professor said. "I should very much like to have you go with me, Rebecca." At no time did he hint at the fact of William Procter as being anywhere in existence.

"I'll go with you, Father," Rebecca answered slowly.

They went to Capstone first, and after staying two days on the business of the mines, they took the train for Pyramid. The two camps were not far apart, and the professor and Rebecca expected to reach Pyramid in the afternoon. But there was a wreck of ore cars on the railroad, and the train was delayed several hours.

Arriving at last in Pyramid, the professor and Rebecca walked up the board sidewalk of the main street toward the best hotel. There was an unusually large crowd on the streets, and to the two of them coming from the scholastic quiet and refinement of Andover, there was a bewildering amount of noise and shouting and confusion. Every saloon and gambling house of the camp was running, open and alive with raucous activity. Every now and then, a revolver shot was heard. The camp had started in on one of its wild, reckless nights, and while those familiar with its nightlife were more or less prepared for its turmoil, the effect of it on strangers was startling. A light rain was softly falling, and the professor held a tight grip on his umbrella, as if he meant to use it as a weapon of defense in case he was held up.

"This is not the place for you, Rebecca," said the professor, as she clung to his arm a little tighter and shrank back as they passed saloon after saloon.

"I'm not afraid," said Rebecca, and it was true that the strange sights had the effect of provoking her to a courage she really did not possess.

As she spoke, they suddenly came to a crowd of people gathered in front of a large building. Above the doorway, there was a cloth sign announcing that preaching services were being conducted inside.

*This must be the place where William is working*, said Rebecca to herself. Before she knew it, she and her father were in the mob of people pouring into the hall.

"Shall we step in a moment and see what sort of a meeting is going on here?" the professor said.

Rebecca murmured something in assent, and in a few moments the two found themselves caught in the jam of the crowd and were being carried into the hall. The majority were miners, but there were a few women. The professor tightened his hold of his umbrella. Someone jostled him roughly, nearly knocking his hat off his head. At last, he and Rebecca were inside the room and fairly pushed into seats about two-thirds of the way from the front. It happened that the seats were next to the wide aisle leading up to the platform.

The room was brilliantly lighted. Light was one of the things that Pyramid lavished with an unsparing hand, and William Procter knew its value in a place of preaching as well as in a gambling house. He had already come upon the platform with another man and began to speak while the crowd was still coming in. He had, at last, made a convert, and he was a powerful one, for he had been a professional gambler, well known to every other gambler in the camp. His conversion was a miraculous event, and he was as eager to save life now as he had been to destroy it before.

So William, rejoicing in such an ally as this, had brought him in this night to illustrate the gambler's tricks. The ex-gambler had brought with him a complete set of his old gambling apparatuses, and he set them all out on the front of the platform. After a simple account of his conversion, he showed the crowd how helpless the young men were in the hands of the professional gambler.

For a half hour, the crowd was fascinated by the sight of this professional gambler and the demonstration he made with his skillful manipulation of cards and dice. The audience remained quiet, breathlessly watching and listening.

Then suddenly, someone in the rear of the hall fired a revolver toward the stage. The plaster fell down from the wall just above William's head where the bullet had struck. Instantly, shouts came from throughout the audience: "No shooting! … Put your gun away! … Calm down!"

In the midst of all the confusion, the converted gambler stood calmly by his table waiting for a chance to be heard. William dusted the plaster from his coat sleeve and remained seated. And it seemed as if the confusion would die down when everyone was startled by the sight of a tall figure in black, with a lady on his arm, pushing down the aisle toward the platform.

The professor was alarmed. He saw one of his old seminary students in peril and did not intend to sit quietly still and have him shot at. Waving his umbrella and saying something in a loud voice, he dragged Rebecca up on the platform and then turned around in front of William.

William rose, and as he did so, another revolver shot rang out. The professor swung his umbrella like a baseball bat, as if he thought to ward off the bullet by hitting it, and the shot struck a lamp on the table and put out the light. The whole crowd of men in the hall rose, and a tremendous scene of confusion at once began.

Above all the din and noise, one voice rose clear and distinct: "Don't shoot the lady!" It was William's voice, and he pushed Rebecca behind him as he shouted.

But Rebecca the next moment turned and looked up at him. Even amidst the shouting and commotion, William heard her say, "Never again will we be apart."

William couldn't help but smile at the irony of the situation—a tender, romantic moment as a near brawl swirled around them. Nevertheless, he wasn't going to let the opportunity pass.

Bending close to Rebecca's ear, he asked, "Do you mean, Rebecca, that you will stay with me forever?"

"Yes," she replied immediately.

And after that, William did not seem to care about anything else. He looked out over the mob in the hall, where fights were erupting, and huddled close to Rebecca to shield her from harm. He prayed for the safety of the woman who had in this bewildering manner been restored to his life after the long, heartbreaking silence of days and nights of sorrow.

22.

# Rebecca Surrenders

❦

EVENTUALLY, THE DISTURBANCE in the hall died down and order was restored. The people began to take their seats, ready for the service to resume. William, after he had seen Rebecca safely to her seat, came to the front of the platform. His converted friend picked up his presentation where he'd left off and, when he had finished, William commented on the gambler's exhibition.

As he went on, William knew that, for the first time since the meetings began, he really had the crowd's full attention. How could he help preaching the best he knew when in the audience sat the woman he loved—the one who had said only a few minutes before that she was willing to share her life with him forever? With an inspiration born of that knowledge, he went on to make a passionate appeal that filled the heart of Rebecca with pride for him.

After the crowd had left the hall, it was somewhat late, but the professor invited William to come to the hotel and have some supper with him and Rebecca. And soon enough, William was seated at a table with his visitors.

"Do you always speak under fire?" asked Professor Phillips.

"No, not always," replied William, laughing. "The meeting tonight was more exciting than usual." He looked at Rebecca as he spoke, and she knew he was not referring to the shooting.

"Yes, I should think it might be a good school of experience for some of our young preachers in the seminary," the professor said. "But if the average congregation shot at the preacher every time they heard something they didn't like, don't you think it would have a tendency to discourage a young preacher somewhat?"

"I should think it might," replied William, laughing even more heartily. "He would always be sure of a wide-awake congregation, however. That would be some gain, wouldn't it?"

Later, when William went back to his boardinghouse that night, he carried with him the professor's promise to visit the reduction mills the next morning. Rebecca wanted to see everything and had told William that she especially wanted to see the place where his accident occurred.

So the next morning, the three visited together several of the famous mines of Pyramid and finally came up to the Golconda mine. William was on very good terms with the superintendent, and he had no trouble getting his guests into the mill. Soon, all three were standing in the doorway looking into the furnace room and at the two mixers as they rolled steadily around on their endless track.

They had been standing there but a moment when the professor wandered away to inspect something, leaving Rebecca and William alone.

"Tell me all about it, William," said Rebecca, as she stood watching the grim machines as they crashed alternately into and out of the roaring furnace.

It was not a morbid curiosity on her part, but she had felt as if she had been deprived of hearing from William's own mouth the terrible incident that could've easily ended his life. So he told her all about it, going into detail regarding Francis Randall's heroic actions. The mention of his name caused Rebecca to ask a question.

"Didn't I hear somewhere that he will soon be called to one of the large churches in New York?" she asked.

"I haven't heard of it," said William. "He is in New York now. I had a letter from him a few days ago, but it was brief and he didn't mention a church. By the way, my sister, Jane, sent me a copy of his book."

"Jane!" cried Rebecca. The two had crossed through the furnace room and were now standing by the open door on the other side, the door through which Francis had stepped to rescue William. "Did I tell you she sent me the newspaper telling about your accident, but not a word of your recovery? And then she answered Father's telegram and addressed it to me."

After that, they stood in the doorway looking out at the wonderful panorama of mountains. The professor was staying a long time in the chemical room, his curiosity aroused by the fascinating sights and smells.

"What are you going to do out here, William?" Rebecca asked shyly.

"I don't know exactly," replied William slowly.

"Will you keep on with the meetings?"

"What do you think I ought to do?" asked William, looking into Rebecca's eyes and seeing the answer there.

"You are in danger ..." Rebecca faltered a bit, but quickly regained her resolute tone. "If you feel called to minister here, though, you must carry on."

"I have thought some of going back to Andover," said William with a pause. Rebecca's face turned rosy red, but she made no answer.

"I must do something to provide for myself. When these meetings here are over, I shall be entirely out of means, Rebecca," William continued with a frankness that she liked in him better than any other quality. "The fact is, my experience out here has shown me my need of thorough preparation if I am going to continue preaching."

"Do you mean that you are going back into the ministry?" asked Rebecca suddenly.

William looked at her and knew he must be truthful, even if it meant losing Rebecca again.

"No, Rebecca," he said, his voice trembling as he said it. "No, I have not decided that I can work best in a church. But my experiences here have taught me that I cannot stand silently by when so many people have never heard—or understood—about salvation in Christ. I cannot say for certain that I will become a minister, but I must serve God wholeheartedly in some way. And I realize I need more training and preparation. If I go back to Andover, I can finish my studies."

Rebecca did not say anything at first, and William took her hand.

He faced her and said, "Rebecca, whether I do my work of preaching in a church or in someplace like last night, is your promise good—will you share your life with me?"

"Yes," replied Rebecca, looking up at him with tear-filled eyes. "Yes, I will go with you and work with you anywhere."

The professor suddenly stepped through the doorway and said, "This is a very fine view out here."

"It certainly is," said William, but he was not looking at the mountains.

"What do you think, Rebecca?" asked the professor with a twinkle of the eyes. "Don't you enjoy it more than the scenery around Andover?"

"Yes, Father, I think I do," and then Rebecca laughed. After a moment, William and the professor joined her.

Two days later when the professor and Rebecca said good-bye to William and started back to Andover, William had talked over matters with the professor and decided to return to the seminary in time for the fall term. He would finish his meetings in Pyramid and then spend the summer earning money to help him during the seminary year.

The last thing the professor said as the train moved away was, "Don't get shot, William. We have need of you in some pulpit!"

# 23.
# THE MARKHAM UNION

❦

HE CHRISTIAN COMMUNITY IN Markham entered summer facing a coming conflict that had the potential to severely test the strength of the church union that had begun so well. In the first place, the organization of the new Christian daily newspaper proved to be a task of tremendous difficulty. Naturally enough, the existing paper in Markham fought for its own life.

But at last, in spite of all challenges and setbacks, the new paper was started. Politically the paper was nonpartisan, representing whatever was for the best good of all the people, and in recognition of the fact that there were good people and good ideas in all the parties.

Then there was the effort to close the saloons and other drinking establishments in Markham. It was clearly understood from the beginning by every subscriber that the paper stood firmly against the sale of alcohol. There was to be no compromise, no temporizing, nothing but the complete prohibition of the saloons as an institution. The election for mayor and council would be held in the fall, and the new paper began with its first issue to map out a plan to help elect officials with high moral and religious character.

The whiskey interests had always taken every previous effort of the Christian community as more or less of a joke. The few lonesome voices raised against it in one church or another had never alarmed purveyors of alcohol in the least. The saloons understood perfectly well that the churches of Markham were divided, and especially of no account in any combined effort in the way of votes. There was not a minister in Markham, before the union movement had begun, who had any influence whatever with his church members when it came to votes. The church member might respect his pastor and even love him greatly, yet if the minister urged him to vote against the saloons, he never dreamed of doing anything of the kind if the vote meant going against the wishes of his party. The fact is, that up to the time when the churches began to come together to overthrow the saloons, Markham had been run on a strictly partisan basis, and not even professed Christian discipleship had changed a man's political action in the matter of votes, when his own party was in danger of defeat.

The year's events, however, had done wonders to invigorate the involvement and determination of Christians in Markham. The Holy Spirit, which had moved so strongly the hearts of Charles Harris and Dean Randall and Mr. Brown, had wrought this transformation upon many businessmen and church members. The publishing of the new Christian paper brought men of different parties together closer than ever before and made possible the campaign against the alcohol sellers, who now began to realize that something unusual was taking place.

A brief conversation between two men who had financial interests in saloons in Markham will give some idea of the impact of the paper. The two men lived in Columbus, where they had large brewery interests, and they sublet to saloons in different towns, Markham among them.

"Noticed this new paper from Markham?" asked one of the brewers of the other, as he took up a copy of *The Markham Union* that had in some way come into the office.

"No. What about it?"

"Why, there's a new paper started in opposition to *The Markham Journal.* The strange thing about it is that it's run completely by church members."

"That so?" asked the other man indifferently, as he lit a cigar.

"Look here!" the first man continued a little roughly. "It may be a more serious matter than you think. The new paper seems to have it in for the saloons, and they're campaigning pretty hard."

"So what?" the second fellow said. "Sounds like another paltry religious outcry against the rum traffic."

"No," replied his companion irritably. "It's more than that. You don't seem to catch on to this. Every church in Markham, including the Catholic church, is a shareholder in this paper, and every minister is an editor. Some of the best businessmen in the place are subscribers and supporters of it, and here in this first number they declared that one of the first objects of the paper is to run the saloons out of

Markham. This is not just a sermon or a set of resolutions against our businessmen. This is a daily paper. Do you realize that fact?"

The truth of the matter began to dawn on the other man, who said, "Gimme the paper." He looked it over carefully and his face began to take on a more serious look.

"We need to look sharp. How much have we invested in Markham?"

The other man made a rapid calculation, "Fifteen saloons, say an average of twelve hundred apiece. About twenty thousand dollars. To say nothing of stock on hand and furnishings. Can you run up to Markham in a day or two and look over matters?"

"Have to, I suppose. The churchpeople must have struck a new deal to get together like this. Suppose they'll vote together when it comes election time, eh?"

"If they do, it'll be the first time," replied the other man gloomily. "But if they can get together to run a daily paper like that, there's no telling what may happen. Curse Markham, anyway! It's always been one of our most profitable towns. Lucky none of the other towns have been struck with this church union craze!"

That week one of them made a visit to Markham, stayed two days, and brought back a gloomy report of the outlook there.

"Fact is, we've got a big fight on our hands if we stay in Markham. Seemed as if nearly the whole town was solid against us. I went to see Father Morris, the Catholic priest. I heard he was trying to build a chapel adjoining the church, and I learned that they were pretty hard up, money coming in slow. I offered to put up a cool thousand or so on condition that he keep still on the saloon question, and, well, I came very near to being kicked out of the house. You never saw such a rage in a Catholic priest anywhere. Somehow, the whole town seems changed. They say it's the result of their church union.

"Why, even the Episcopal dean hobnobs with the Methodist and Baptist and other brethren, as if they were all alike. While I was there, one of the old men who has been preaching in one of the little churches died, and it was common talk on the street that the church would not call a new man but go in with some other church." The man shook his head and continued. "I almost looked to see angels flying around the streets on Sunday. No open post office, hardly any traffic on the streets, no cigar stores or fruit stores going, no drug stores opened, except two hours, and then they wouldn't sell anything but medicine. It was just plain strange, I tell you. Give me a drink of something to wash the sanctimoniousness of Markham out of my system."

He reached out a hand for a bottle on the table, and his companion looked at him dourly.

"Sanctimoniousness is very well if you want to call names, but is it the sort that votes as it prays?" the man said. "That's all we care for. If it is, we might as well close up shop in Markham."

"I think we might as well," said the man who had been to Markham. "The game is up there, but we'll fight it out just the same."

24.

# True Christian Unity

❦

O WHEN FALL CAME, MARKHAM was the scene of a whiskey war that raged as fiercely as any political contest ever fought in the state. But the saloon and alcohol proprietors, for the first time, faced a solidly united church—united not simply to denounce saloons, but to put them out of business with a united vote in the election.

Added to this fact was the influence of the Christian newspaper, which entered the homes of the people every morning and soon became recognized as the champion of righteousness. The saloon men hated and feared *The Markham Union*. As much as they might have scoffed at prayer meetings and sermons and church programs, they could not scoff at what was actually visible in type.

In all this work of the churches, Francis Randall had a prominent part, even though he had been in New York longer than he had planned. He made arrangements with his publisher for another book, and on his way back to Markham he outlined the details of the story. But his thoughts were more than ever filled with Jane. Should he speak to her when he got home?

The second day after his return, he was obliged to consult John Procter about some detail of church work, and after a little hesitation he went over to the parsonage. He generally avoided John Procter's house in order to escape the embarrassment of seeing Jane. Now he hoped he would see her. It was nearly dusk when Francis called, and John was in his study.

The two men were discussing a new program when John excused himself to retrieve some papers from another room. As Francis sat there waiting for his host's return, he overheard Kate and Jane talking in the next room. He thought he heard his name mentioned and, not wanting to eavesdrop on the conversation, stood to let them know he was there.

Before he could say anything, however, he clearly heard Jane say, "Oh, Mother, I regret ever making that foolish speech about the trials of being a poor minister's daughter. It seems so immature now, and I fear I've lost Francis forever."

Francis stood transfixed, wondering whether to reveal his presence or simply remain silent.

As he was working this out in his mind, Kate said, "But I am sure Francis still loves you. He came every day to inquire about you while you were ill, and I heard he was seen many times standing at the corner looking up at the room. Young men don't do that on bitter nights unless they care deeply for someone. And, in fact, Jane, he told me that he still loved you. That was at the first of your illness!"

There was a silence of a moment, and Francis would have given a good deal to see Jane's face just then. Walking toward the open doorway, he once again stopped short when Jane spoke again.

"Don't you see my dilemma, Mother? I told him I didn't want to marry a poor minister. I'm sure I appeared very silly, making such a big deal about money. But now it looks as if he'll have plenty of money from the sales of his book. If I rekindle our relationship, how can I make him know it is genuinely because of my love for him and not because of his money?"

"I believe you just did," Francis said, stepping out of the study.

Jane gasped, while her mother's eyes grew wide with surprise.

"How long have you been in there?" Jane said in a voice that conveyed both anger and hope. "How much did you hear?"

"I wasn't trying to eavesdrop," he said apologetically. "I was waiting for your father to return."

Jane stammered, "I, well, I was just telling Mother ..."

"I know," he said. "I heard all you said. Is it true? Do you still love me?"

Kate cleared her throat and, leaving the room, whispered, "Excuse me—I need to check on dinner."

Francis took a step toward Jane and said, "If I understood rightly, you think I might be rich from the sale of my books. And you would not marry me now for fear I might think you are marrying for money and perhaps fame. Is that right, Jane? If I can prove to you that I am still comparatively poor, and not famous enough to hurt anybody, will you marry me?"

Jane entered the study and sat down. This girl who rarely hesitated to speak seemed speechless.

Francis said again, "If I prove that I am not and probably never will be rich from the sale of my books, will you marry me?"

"That is not what I said," answered Jane, somewhat indistinctly.

"Nevertheless, I can easily prove it to you," he said. "I shall be safe in saying that even if the book had a constant sale for years, I could never make much from it. The fact is, the terms I agreed to with the publisher were tilted greatly in their favor—not mine. Though the book has sold well, my royalties won't amount to anything great, even if it continues to sell. Besides which, I've felt compelled to give away most of the earnings from the book. I am afraid—or not afraid, actually—that I am nearly as poor as ever."

Jane rose to her feet under an impulse she could not define, and Francis rose also and stood beside her. A tear started down her cheek. She turned her face toward her lover, and the next instant he held her in his arms and she was sobbing out something on his shoulder.

Suddenly, John Procter's voice sounded from the hallway.

"Excuse me, Francis, for keeping you waiting so long,"

he said, but as he came into the study and saw how matters stood, he quickly retreated to the sitting room. As he hurried off, he called, "Never mind. Our business can wait for another day."

When she was sure her father had gone, Jane said, "There is one thing, Francis. I am a little troubled about something." She smiled slyly, and he knew she was being coy. "You know I said many times I would never marry a minister. So if I promise to marry you, am I not breaking a promise to myself?"

He knew she was teasing with him. "I don't think I can help you out of that difficulty, my dear," he said. "In fact, I am going to do my best to make you break that promise to yourself. It is better broken than kept."

"Ah, I see a way out of it," continued Jane. "You are not *only* a minister. You are an author as well."

"So that's the way you deal with your conscience?" cried Francis, laughing. And then he added as Jane looked up at him, "Minister or author or whatever else I may be, you love me for myself, don't you, Jane?"

"Yes," replied Jane. "And I would love you just the same if you were but a minister and poor and unknown, instead of an author—whose future books may or may not pay handsomely."

Jane laughed lightly again, and for both of them the whole world grew young again in the light of the best thing in it, after their winter of darkness and sorrow.

When they went into the sitting room, Kate was bringing supper into the next room where John was reading the newspaper. He looked up with a smile.

Kate came to the door between the two rooms. "We'll be

glad to have you join our family circle for supper," she said, beaming on the two.

John added, "Yes, indeed, I think you ought to stay."

Francis looked at Jane, and they both sat down without a word.

After several minutes, while food was dished out, Francis broke the silence. "It seems as if I will join the family circle not only for one meal, but for many meals. In fact, we'll be sharing meals throughout our lifetime."

The next minute, Jane was caught and kissed by her mother.

John sprung up and shook Francis by the hand warmly. It is safe to say that there were not four happier people at any supper table in Markham that night than those in the old Congregational parsonage.

25.

# A Christmas Wedding

❦

FOUR MONTHS LATER, ON Christmas Day, Jane Procter and Francis Randall were married. It was Jane's wish to be married at the family's parsonage, for that is where they were reunited after many months apart. As for Francis, he said he would've been more than happy to marry Jane anywhere on Earth.

So, on that bright Christmas night, with wreaths of holly and evergreen adorning the room, the couple stood near the large hearth fireplace, with the room crowded with friends and family members. There, John pronounced Jane and Francis man and wife in the name of the Father and the Son and the Holy Ghost.

A week later, on New Year's Day, John received a letter from William announcing the fact that he had definitely decided to do his lifework through the ministry of the church. He wrote,

> I have reached this decision, dear Father, after coming back to the seminary. I believe I can serve best by being in line with the established organization—though you know I will not settle for the old way of doing things. I shall always be pressing for new and better ways to serve people and show them God's love.
>
> Next June, Rebecca and I shall be married, and we will be ready to enter any field where we may be called. I thank God for all the ways He has led me, and most of all for the extraordinary life partner He has given me.

John finished reading and walked to the window. He recalled vividly reading another letter from his son in that very study—a letter, he had to admit, that caused him much disappointment. That's when his son announced he was leaving seminary and pursuing other opportunities besides full-time ministry … maybe forever.

Amazing how God had worked in the lives of so many people, his son perhaps most of all!

He looked out upon the town as it lay white and still under its cover of snow. He could still count several church steeples, though his own was not among the number. But he breathed a prayer of thanksgiving to think that now the churches of Markham moved under a common impulse for one purpose.

*It could be, William, that God will call you to serve here*, John thought.

And then he said, very quietly, as he looked out upon his town, "But wherever God calls you, William, work to bring about unity among believers and among churches. God's work will be accomplished more powerfully through unified followers of Christ. I once thought I'd never see such a miracle of grace as that which has occurred in Markham. But God and His Spirit are at work in our world—as mightily as ever. If only Christians will devote themselves to one another and be united in heart and spirit, a great revival will sweep over the earth."

In the spirit of hope and thanksgiving, John looked out upon the town and prayed that the new year might witness in every town and city of the world the same events that people had begun to call "The Miracle at Markham."

Additional copies of Charles Sheldon's classic
*Miracle at Markham*
are available wherever good books are sold.

❦

If you have enjoyed this book, or if it has had
an impact on your life,
we would like to hear from you.

Please contact us at

RIVEROAK BOOKS
Cook Communications Ministries, Dept. 201
4050 Lee Vance View
Colorado Springs, CO 80918

Or visit our Web site
www.cookministries.com